Bedlam: A Twisted Hearts Love Story

Copyright © Autumn Sand 2017

eBook ISBN 978-0-9967954-1-8

Cover design by Pixel Mischief

Edited by All About The Edits

Proofread and Formatted by The Last Step Proofreading

## Disclaimer

Dear Reader,

As the author of this book I want to warn readers that there is rape and violence against women in the subject matter. Though I do not condone these acts, they unfortunately exist in this world. I do not in anyway glamorize the portrayals of these acts of violence but I do show how there is life after.

Thank you,

Autumn Sand

## Twisted Hearts Love Stories

What is Twisted Hearts? For me this series is about overcoming obstacles in life and finding true love. It is never letting life get you down. No matter what comes your way you remain hopeful for that happy ending. It is finding strength within yourself while learning to accept help from others.

This series is also meant to be a fast-paced thrill ride while touching on hard subjects.


This is from one hopeful soul to another, read this if you dare.

*Autumn*

# Chapter 1
## Heartbreak Hotel ~ Whitney Houston feat. Faith Evans & Kelly Price

*Ugh! What is that annoying sound?* I come out of my dream, slowly opening my tired eyes, and stare at the object of my irritation. My alarm clock. That damn thing must be broken; there is no way it's six a.m. How dare it disturb me, ripping me from my dream of Bradley Cooper and me on a beautiful, sunny beach?

I slap the fool machine and give it an angry glare. Mark one for mankind against the machine. Stretching in my king-size bed, I realize the right side is empty. I wish I could muster the energy to care that he didn't bother to come home last night, or at least call to say he wasn't. I'm so past the stage of staying up at night, crying over him, wishing he'd come home to me. I stretch again for good measure, before getting up to start my daily routine.

I walk to my floor-to-ceiling windows and open the curtains to an awesome view of the city skyline.

Ignacio and I own a penthouse in a very chic section of Manhattan. It's in one of those trendy boutique buildings where they cater to your every whim. Initially, Ignacio balked at the price, but now he enjoys all the luxuries the building offers. Well, he enjoys them when he decides to actually come home.

I drag my feet across the plush carpeting toward the master bathroom, and take my shower, the radio on full blast. Singing in the shower is my favorite thing to do. Okay, it's actually my second favorite; my first would be grabbing cocktails with my best friend, Rheda.

One of Pink's latest songs begins to play, and I belt out the words as if I had written them myself. If you ask me, I sound just like her when I sing. If you ask someone else, they'll say I sound like a wounded animal. That's the problem with opinions these days; everyone has one.

I pour a large glob of my beloved body wash from Bath and Body Works, Sea Island Cotton, onto my loofa and lather up. The scent wafts up to my nose and fills the shower with its delicious aroma. I am instantly rejuvenated. All I need is a cup of joe, or a guy named one, and this will officially be a kickass morning. The radio jockey announces the time and I realize I've stayed a little too long at the party, so I finish showering and dry off quickly.

I've never been one of those people who choose their outfit ahead of time. I'm more of an "in the moment" type of girl, letting my mood choose the clothes. I step inside my walk-in closet which, if you asked my boyfriend, is just a miniature boutique in itself. I go through the painstaking process of choosing the look of the day. You know that look that says either, "Hey, don't fuck with me" or "Hey, I'm sexy and I know it." I'm feeling in between the spectrum, so I choose a dove gray Chanel pant suit, with Louboutin stilettos to complete the look. I love my hooker heels; they give me the extra height I lack in my five-foot-one-inch frame.

I work for one of the top interior designers in New York, so I must always look the part. It's a dog-eat-dog world in this industry. You need every edge you can get, and looking like the best is crucial.

Glancing at my reflection in the floor-length mirror, I admire myself. My dark hair falls naturally around my shoulders in loose curls. When I was a child, my wide brown eyes looked too large for my delicate face, but as an adult, I grew in all the right places. Most find my eyes appealing. Drawing my eyes away from the mirror, I check the time; it's eight o'clock. Perfect! I still have time to read the morning paper over a cup of coffee.

I walk through the house and into our sleek, modern kitchen, decorated in white and pewter. I personally picked out each and every item when we were remodeling, even the faucet and handles. Too bad I rarely cook in here. It's not that I don't know how, I just never find a reason to. Ignacio is never home, and on the rare occasion he is, we go out to eat. So, ordering in is usually my late-night meal go-to. Ignacio has yet to complain—oh wait, that's right. He's never home *to* complain.

I turn on my Keurig and wait for the indicator to tell me the water's hot. I know it only takes thirty seconds, but it feels like an eternity is holding me back from yummy goodness. I hear the slam of the front door, which would be my boyfriend, announcing his arrival in his own special way. I close my eyes briefly, wishing I had opted for Starbucks instead. Instinctively, I grab another cup because I'm sure he'll ask for one anyway. The little blue light on my Keurig blinks, ready to give me the nectar of the gods. As I begin my quick brewing process, Ignacio walks into the kitchen. He looks tired and rumpled. Probably exhausted and tore up by some hellcat he slept with. He reeks of expensive perfume and cigarettes. Knowing he isn't a smoker, either the woman he was with is or he has recently taken up the habit.

Walking up behind me, he grabs me around my waist and kisses me on my cheek.

"Knew I would find you," he murmurs as he kisses his way down my neck. It's a game we used to play with each other when we had some semblance of a relationship. It started when we first met. I was running down the street, late for work at my after-school job, and ran smack into him. He caught me in time before I landed flat on my ass. He made a joke and said, "I knew you would find me." It eased my embarrassment, and we've been together ever since. We haven't said that to each other in years, and now, here I am, fighting the urge to wipe away the feel of his wet, fraudulent kiss. I fix his cup of coffee and place it in front of him. Grabbing another pod from the rack, I brew my own.

With my steaming cup of salvation, I sit at the kitchen island and turn on my tablet to read the *New York Times*.

*Slurp.* "Ahh." *Slurp.* "Ahh."

I cringe inwardly at him slurping away at his coffee. He needs to do two things. First, stop slurping; second, take a shower.

"You're quiet this morning. You on your period or something?" he asks in a groggy voice.

I wince at his words. How dare he question why I'm quiet. Fuck him! I look up from my tablet and into his bloodshot green eyes. His dark brown hair is tousled, no doubt from the tramp who ran her fingers through it as they were having sex. I used to think I was the luckiest girl in the world to have him. Back then, he was the absolute catch, and I was the envy of all the girls. Now, I wish I could throw this fish back in the water and go fishing for another.

"Who? Me? I don't think I'm particularly quiet." I try to take some of the edge out of my voice, but he gives me a look anyway. Guess I'm not earning any Academy Award nominations anytime soon.

He stares at me warily. "What's your day looking like?" he asks in between slurps. God, can I slap him? Or at least slap the cup out of his hand?

"Busy." Yep, that's the best he'll get out of me this morning. I return my concentration to the article I'm reading.

"Hell, you're always busy." He has a lot of nerve to complain. He never has to sit at home alone and wake up to an empty bed.

"Well, since I got my promotion, Chelsea has given me more clients. I'm still trying to earn my name in the industry." I take a final swallow from my cup and stand to place it in the dishwasher.

"*Humph.* Your career is more important than taking care of your man?" He shoves his mug away,

11

and coffee sloshes onto the table as we glare at one another.

"Take care of you? Iggy, you would have to come home every now and then for me to do that." I slam the dishwasher door harder than I intend, and the dishes inside clink around. Bracing my hands on the counter, I close my eyes to reel in my temper.

"Da fuck I wanna come home to? This shit?" His hands slam on the table, rattling everything, including my nerves. He stands, abruptly knocking his chair to the ground in a loud thud. A large indentation appears on the bottom of the wall, as well as in our relationship.

I let out a yelp and jerkily place both hands on my chest. "Never mind, Iggy. Just never fucking mind." I run my shaky hands through my hair. We haven't been able to have a conversation in months, without it going straight to an argument.

"What does that mean? 'Never mind?'" Spittle comes out of his mouth as his eyes narrow. When did he stop loving me? Or I him?

I exhale loudly as my heart thunders in my chest. "It means I don't want to argue." *It means I don't know why I stay anymore.*

"What do you want? A ring? I asked you before, and you said no. You change your mind?"

He didn't ask me before, he told me. Not so romantic when your boyfriend is close to an orgasm and he tells you, *"We should fucking get married,"* just before he explodes in your mouth. I gag at the memory and turn to grab a bottled water from the fridge.

"It's been eleven years, so I guess it's time to make it legal. We can go to the courts or something."

"Twelve," I say through gritted teeth as I slam my bottled water on to the counter. I need a goddamn aspirin. I grab my Birkin to search for one.

"What?" His forehead puckers as if he is trying to solve a *New York Times* crossword puzzle.

I turn to face him with the bottle of Aleve in hand, pointing it in his direction. "Twelve years. We've been together for twelve years, Iggy." *If we're going to argue about something, then at least get the fucking*

13

*details right, asshole.* I turn my back to him and try desperately to open the bottle.

"Oh."

Realizing I just don't have the energy to open the bottle, or argue anymore, I throw the pain reliever back in my bag and turn, glaring at him. "It's not about a ring, Iggy. It never has been. It's about you giving me the respect of asking me and not telling me. I'm not one of your men, jumping at your orders." I'm, of course, referring to the criminal empire he runs. Iggy is head of the DeLuca crime family. If you watch those Mafia documentary television shows, you would have caught an episode about his father, Mario DeLuca.

"I think I know the difference between you and my guys. I don't fuck them," he says with a smirk that spreads wide across his face.

Well, that isn't saying anything. There really isn't much difference between me and his men since he doesn't fuck me, either. "Never mind, Iggy. I have to go." I turn to leave, exasperated with this conversation.

"Yo, I won't be home tonight," he calls out to me as I'm leaving the kitchen.

"Thanks," I say, actually sincere in my gratitude.

"For what?"

"For at least telling me in advance that you'll not be home with me, but in some whore's bed instead. So, thanks for the heads-up." I exit the same way he entered, with a slam of the front door.

I leave the penthouse and that argument behind me, taking our private elevator down to the ornate lobby.

"Good morning, Fred," I say to our doorman.

As usual, he is watching the news with his feet up behind his desk. When he hears my voice, he turns the volume down and stands up, straightening his uniform. Walking around the desk, he gives a slight bow. No, he doesn't have to. He's just old school that way.

"Good mawnin', Mrs. DeLuca." His southern drawl is so cute and charming, it makes me want to protect him from the big bad city.

In all the years we've been here, I've never bothered to correct him. I am not a Mrs., but instead I am Ms. Ms. Scott, to be exact.

He steps ahead of me to get the door, and I walk out into the humid summer air. "So, what's on the news this morning?" This is our little thing. Every morning, as he hails a cab for me, he will give me an update on the current events. Fred, I've found, is very well versed on all current events, be it local or global.

"Mrs. DeLuca, you know it's the same crap." He leans in as if this was for my ears only in a city of millions. "Congress didn't approve that bill for the veterans." He shakes his head as if he'd just heard a neighbor's fifteen-year-old pet dog just died. His fingers wrap around his silver whistle and he rolls it between his fingertips. Letting out a deep exhale, he lifts the whistle to his lips and blows, waving his hand to a taxi down the street. "I tell you, those jokers don't know what they're doing."

I wipe a bead of sweat from my brow and laugh. I love these conversations with him. "Fred, you should run for office. Set 'em straight." I'm actually serious when I say this, but he laughs as he opens the cab door for me, waiting for me to get in.

"Mrs. DeLuca, they wouldn't know what to do with an old veteran like me. Nah. I'm happy with what I do. I get to meet nice people and the hours are pretty decent." He prattles off my work address to the driver.

I take a seat in the cab, which I immediately realize does not have air conditioning. "Fred, I would vote for you. We need more people like you in office."

"Well, if I should ever change my mind, Mrs. DeLuca, I'll count on your vote. Have a good day." He closes the door and waves at me as the cab departs.

The heat in the cab is overwhelming, even with the windows rolled down. "Excuse me. Can you turn on the air?"

"No. No air," the cab driver snaps angrily. I'm not sure if he's mad I asked the question or mad because it's so hot you can fry an egg on the leather seats, so I decide to leave it alone.

I lean my head back on the seat, praying for the pounding in my head to subside, but it's just getting worse. Shitty start to my day, thanks to Iggy. Twelve years together and I don't think there is an ounce of love left between us. I'm starting to wonder if we ever loved each other, or if we're addicted to tearing each other down. I stay because he is, after all, the only family I've ever really had.

I've come a long way from my wretched beginnings as a product of the foster care system. By time I turned five, both of my parents were dead from drug overdoses. I'll never forget the morning I woke up and found my father with a needle in his arm, slumped over the toilet. I thought he was sleeping and tried to wake him, but he never did.

*"Daddy. Daddy. Please, wake up, Daddy."* I kept shaking him, repeating it, until I was hoarse and the tears could no longer fall. His body was cold to the touch and had an eerie pallor. I removed the needle and placed it in his bedroom where he kept his other drug

paraphernalia. Eventually, a neighbor called the cops, because she heard my cries through the paper-thin walls.

My childhood with my parents never consisted of outings at parks or playdates with other kids. I was usually with them when they made their drug buys, and my mother taught me how to put her "medicine" in the syringe by time I was three. That was the year she died. Her overdose was on a train and it took several hours before anyone realized she was dead. My father was too high at the time to understand what the police were telling him, when they came to our house to tell him that mommy was never coming home. We never had a real funeral for her because my father couldn't afford one. She ended up in what they call Potters Field. That's the place they bury the unwanted. Or at least, that's how I've always looked at it.

My parents had no family to speak of, so I was bounced from foster home to foster home, never really having a sense of belonging or being loved. I guess that's why I've stayed with Iggy for so long. He's the only constant thing in my life.

The memories of my past hits me in waves, and a loud sob escapes my mouth.

"Lady, you okay back there?"

I cough, attempting to keep the tears at bay. "Umm, yes. Just had to clear my throat."

As we near my office, I dry my eyes and quickly freshen up my makeup, which is hard to do because the cabbie is driving like a bat out of hell. I step out of the taxi and walk into C.F. Interior Design, the company where I work.

The building has a mix of tenants, ranging from lawyers, doctors, and engineers. Basically, people who overcharge for their services. I wait for the elevator with a few regulars who usually come in at the same time as I do. The ride to the twentieth floor is quick and I say goodbye to the familiar faces that have a few more floors to go.

"C.F. Interior Designs, how may I help you?" Corrine, the receptionist, answers the phone in a singsong voice as I step off the elevator. I wave to her and she gives me a bright smile in return.

I nod at some of my co-workers as I make my way to my office. Having only had this position for six months, my office is still not fully decorated, but I love it just the same. I place my Birkin on the desk, and there's a faint knock on my open door. I look up and see Fran.

"Anaya, you have a full schedule today, as you know. I've sent a detailed rundown of your day to your tablet." Junior designers, such as myself, share Fran as our personal assistant. When you become a full-fledged designer, you get your own. That's a promotion I hope to get within two years.

"Thanks, Fran," I say, as I pick up my tablet to look at my schedule. My argument with Iggy prevented me from checking it before I left this morning.

"Is there anything else you need from me?" she asks from the doorway.

"Yes. Please call Rheda and confirm we're meeting for lunch at Rio."

"No problem," she says and closes the door behind her.

I open my sketchbook and begin the finishing touches on a project I've been working on for one of New York's one percent. The woman who commissioned a redo of her living room and dining room has had one Botox injection too many. I swear her face looks as if it's permanently frozen in place. It's sad, if you ask me. Who wants to go through life with an eternal grin? Not me. I hope I never feel the need to do that to my body. She, unfortunately, also wears clothes too young for her and dyes her hair a hideous dishwater blonde. News flash, honey, looking like a carbon copy of the next best thing will not keep your man home. If he's going to wander, he'll wander. I should know, having my very own wanderer at home, slurping his damn coffee, while sitting in a cloud of some slut's hundred-dollar an ounce scent.

Several meetings and a few cups of coffee later, Fran is back to inform me I'm running late for my lunch with Rheda. I grab my pocketbook and run out the door. Rheda hates it when I'm late.

Rheda is a take-no-prisoners redhead, who is quick-witted and sharp-tongued. I love her, and she's my best friend. She also has the unfortunate distinction of being Ignacio's lawyer. We met through Iggy when he took me to her law firm's client mixer. She and I hit it off immediately. I'd stab a bitch for Rheda, and she would get me off on a technicality.

One of the reasons why I was so drawn to Rheda is because she has known heartache. Her older sister was gang raped and eventually committed suicide while attending college in Oklahoma. Understandably, Rheda was never the same. She changed her major to law and never looked back. After passing the bar, she worked in the District Attorney's office. She eventually moved into private practice; she was tired of all the degenerates and psychos going free, and it soured her against state-run legal farms. She later joined one of New York's most prestigious law firms.

I jump from the cab and run into the restaurant. Well, not *run*. Who runs in Louboutins? The *maître d'* informs me Rheda is already seated and waiting for me. A hostess immediately escorts me to the table, where Rheda takes a sip of her martini as she looks at me with narrowed eyes. That scowl of hers has frazzled many a witness on the stand.

"I swear, darling, you artistic types are never on time," she tells me, once again. My tardiness is a usual point of contention between us.

"Sorry. I got so caught up in work, time just slipped away from me." We air kiss and I take my seat, picking up the menu.

"Don't bother. I've already ordered a few dishes for us. Some of us have to get back to work, you know," she says to me as I hand my menu back to the waiter.

"Did you order my drink as well?" I smirk.

"Nope, I left that decision to you, my dear," she replies, with a careless wave of her hand.

"Jack and Coke," I tell the waiter.

"Honey, I just don't know how you drink that." She scrunches up her nose and shakes her head, her naturally curly hair flapping from side to side.

"I like it. It is rich, dark, and smooth. Just the way I like my men," I joke.

"Speaking of which, whose bed was Papa Bear sleeping in last night?"

"Not mine, that's for sure. I don't even remember the last time we had sex," I pout as I play with my fork.

"You mean, you don't know when the last time *you* had sex was, honey. Because your man is definitely getting it from somewhere else. So, the 'we' is really just *you*."

Leave it to Rheda to tell it like it is. I look around the bustling restaurant as the elite of New York nibble at their wedge salads and the souls of the poor.

"You know what you need?" Rheda asks as she taps her French manicured nails against her martini glass.

"Do tell." My words drip with sarcasm.

"A man. Find yourself a stud, honey. Jump in the saddle and ride him like a horse." She slaps her hand through the air, imitating a rounding slap on her butt.

"I can't do that. Even though he cheats, I just can't bring myself to do the same." It doesn't make sense; I guess I'm a glutton for punishment…and a life I can control. He's doing as Iggy does. It's typical. It's become the norm. I like typical. Normal. In my private life, that is. When it comes to my career, bring on the bigger, better, amaze-tits life experiences.

Rheda places both hands on the table and leans in slightly. "You need to leave him. You're better than this, and you know it."

"I've thought about it, but it all comes down this. If I leave, what will I have? I'm not used to being on my own anymore, and it scares me. Twelve years is a lot to throw away. It's not easily discarded like an ugly fabric swatch or an old piece of pizza. The passionate love is long gone, but I still care about him."

Iggy used to be so loving, so attentive. The best of teenaged boyfriends. I went away to college, his father died, and he took over the family business. I didn't notice right away, but Iggy began to change. I don't know the day and time we lost the flame that made us so strong, but it happened. And I don't think we can get the fire going again.

"Well then, I say find a stud and be done with it." Rheda gives me a wink as she sips on her martini. "By the way, how are the sketches for my bedroom coming along?"

"Not bad. I worked on them briefly this morning. I should have something to show you in the next couple of weeks."

"Good. I can't wait to see them."

I'd do Rheda's sketches. I do whatever I needed to do to stay busy. To have an excuse for leaving Iggy and our dead relationship at the back of my mind. If Iggy wasn't in my bed, I didn't have to *feel* anything.

Speaking of beds…could I do it? Could I really find a stud and ride him like a cowgirl in the state rodeo finals?

Do I dare?

## Chapter 2

## Kashmir ~ Led Zeppelin

It's a few days after my lunch with Rheda, and I'm at my desk working on sketches for a client's restaurant. I have a teeny budget to work with, and it's taking every brain cell in my head to make the numbers and the designs work. Frustrated, I stand and stretch. I walk to my office windows and stare out at the city, daydreaming a bit before I get back to work. A light knock on my office door interrupts my thoughts.

The C.F. in C.F. Interior Designs walks in.

How does one describe Chelsea Faggini? She's a tall, leggy, platinum blonde with a perfect hourglass figure that most women would kill for. When I say most women, I'm including myself. Chelsea, a woman who looks to be in her mid-thirties, but in reality, is in her forties, walks with an air of sensual confidence.

"Ms. Faggini." I immediately straighten my shoulders and try to appear taller than I really am.

"I think it's about time you call me Chelsea." She takes a seat by my client table and crosses her long bronzed legs.

My mouth drops open, before I quickly close it. Since when is she okay with us being on a first name basis? Realizing that she is staring at me, most likely looking like a moron, I take a seat on the opposite side of the round table.

*Think, Anaya, think. Did you turn in all your client sketches on time? Perhaps I missed a meeting?* I'm going over the past few days in my head, when Chelsea pulls me away from my thoughts.

"So, I bet you're wondering why I'm here."

"Umm…" Why am I picking *now* to be tongue-tied? I wipe my sweaty palms on my dress in a guise of straightening it.

"Well, I received a phone call last night, from my good friend, Tony Delaney." She throws the name out with a flutter of the eyes.

Dumbfounded, I give her a blank stare. Why is she telling me about her friends? She never so much as says "Good Morning" to me.

Sitting back in her seat, she arches an eyebrow, clasping her hands in front of her. "You *do* know who Tony Delaney is, don't you?"

My mouth feels like cotton as I sense I'm about to flunk a major test. "I'm sorry. Should I?"

She closes her eyes briefly and shakes her head, before reopening them to give me a wide-eyed stare. Or perhaps, a glare? I shrink a little in my seat.

"He's the owner of Pulse. I'm assuming you've heard of Pulse, haven't you?" Her voice drips sarcasm like a leak in a faucet.

Well hell, who hasn't heard of Pulse? It's the hottest club in the Tri-state Area. I've heard all the rumors about the goings on in that club; the VIP rooms where anything goes. Rheda and I tried checking it out one night. We stood in line for forty minutes but couldn't get in. Rheda said I should've used Ignacio's name, but I didn't want to. I wanted to get in on my own merit, but apparently, that wasn't enough. "Yes, yes I have."

She lets out a sigh. "Then let's continue, shall we? Tony called me last night and wants to hire C.F. Interior Design to redecorate the club."

I move a wayward hair from my face. "Umm, okay." I figuring saying less is more, since I don't know where this is leading.

She leans in closer to the table and places her hands on the edge. Her blood-red nails look like she clawed someone's eyes out for lunch. "Are you sure you don't know him?"

I shake my head.

Her eyes narrow. "Never met him?"

Another head shake.

"Your boyfriend?"

She's got me there. I wouldn't know if Iggy knows this guy or not, so I shrug.

"I don't understand it."

Before I have time to think, my response slips from my mouth. "Don't understand what?"

Did she snarl? I thought only animals did that. Yeah, I think she snarled. I swallow hard and avert my eyes.

"Why on earth did he ask for you specifically?"

My already wide brown eyes must look like they're going to pop right out of my head, as my jaw drops to the ground.

Chelsea rises and paces the floor. "Well, for obvious reasons, I told him that a project like this is not normally handled by a junior designer, but he said he saw a room you decorated at a friend's house in the Hamptons."

That was my first project as a junior designer. It was the family room for the Westwoods. They are old New York money. I'm giddy with excitement that a project I did is getting outside recognition. A larger than life smile spreads across my face. Perhaps I can make full designer *before* my two-year goal.

Chelsea stops in front of me, tapping her pointed shoe. Her arms are folded and she is glaring at me. At least it's not a snarl. "I don't see anything to smile about. You don't have the experience for a project like this, but he insists that it has to be you." Bending down slightly, she points her finger at me. "I don't think I need to tell you what a project like this means to our firm. If you fuck this up, I will toss you out of here on your ass, and you will never work in this town again."

Wow. People actually say,? I always thought that was just in the movies. But I keep my humble opinion to myself and nod in understanding. Appeased, she straightens and fluffs out her platinum locks.

"Does that mean the project is mine?" I croak out.

She huffs and places her hands on her slender waist. "Yes. You have an appointment with the club tomorrow at ten a.m. sharp. I will have Fran move your other clients to the other juniors. I want this to be your main focus. If you can, by some miraculous effort, not fuck it up, then this could possibly mean designing his other clubs in Miami, Vegas, and L.A."

A loud gulp escapes me.

"You can say that again. So, it's show time, sweetheart. Finish up what you are working on, so you can handoff." She turns and walks toward the door but stops, turning around to face me, her hand on the doorknob. "And Anaya?"

I look up, stunned to hear my name from her lips. "*Don't* fuck it up." She opens the door and slams it behind her, causing me to jump in my seat.

Rheda is going to piss in her pants when she finds out! I stand and jump around my office like a kid in a candy store. Oh my God, I have to call Rheda and brag my ass off.

Reaching for my cell on the desk, I hit Rheda's picture and it instantly dials. She answers in a snarky tone but it doesn't rain on my parade.

"Rheda, congratulate me!" I say as I clap, finally letting my excitement spill out.

"Umm…congratulations?"

"I'm at the height of my career. I've been asked to redesign Pulse!" I do yet another happy dance.

"Pulse? As in Pulse, *the* club?" I hear something drop in the background. "How?"

"I don't know, and I don't care. I'm heading there tomorrow to check it out."

"Well, let's go get ripped." I can picture her grabbing her purse, ready to meet me at a bar.

I flop in my chair, suddenly deflated. "Shit. I can't, Rheda. I've got to finish up a project so I can hand it off. Chelsea wants my full attention on Pulse. I might be burning the midnight oil with this one."

"Oh, no worries. We'll celebrate another time." She sounds as bummed as I feel.

"I'll call you after my meeting tomorrow."

"Sounds good. I guess I'd better get back to these briefs I was working on. And Anaya, congratulations."

I smile into the phone. "Aww, thanks, Mama Bear." We both laugh and hang up.

Kicking off my heels, I throw my feet on top of the desk, wiggle my toes, and lean back in my chair. I do an air salute to my kick-ass future.

# Chapter 3
## Crimson and Clover ~ Joan Jett & The Blackhearts

The following day, after my meeting with Chelsea, I stop in front of Pulse and take a look around. The club is located in Manhattan's Meat Packing District. It used to be exactly what the name implies, but as the city changed and the area rezoned from manufacturing to commercial, it became a hip and trendy area. It's perfectly located near four chic hotels with rooftop bars.

I stare at my reflection in the window and straighten my beige dress with the ruffled cap sleeves. It's my favorite Armani. Paired with a brown croc belt and brown croc heels to match, and my favorite perfume, Michael Kors Rose Radiant, I feel sexy and enticing. Knowing that I look the part, I walk to the door and push the buzzer. A tall man with a muscular frame and chiseled features opens the door. He looks me over casually before saying, "The club is closed."

"Hi, I'm Anaya Scott. Tony Delaney is expecting me." I stammer out my words as I try not to stare at this large man.

"Oh yeah, you work for Chelsea. Come in. He's expecting you." He steps aside to let me in.

"I'm sorry. What's your name?"

"Tick." He sounds like Vin Diesel.

Tick? What kind of name is Tick? Did his mother name him that or is that short for something? I open my mouth to ask, but take another look at the imposing man and decide against it.

"Go ahead and do your thing. I'll go find Tony."

I mumble my thanks as I walk through the door and am hit by how different the club looks when the lights are on. Granted, I've never been here before, but I can imagine how it looks when the lights are dim and the music is pumping hypnotic beats. The current theme of the club seems to be glass and glitter, if that could be a theme. Strangely, it works. Whoever did the design was good. I mean, *really* good. So why does he want *me*?

The bar is lengthy, with chandeliers hanging over the long picture framed mirrors. The walls are lined with leather L-shaped booths and VIP tables to give the clientele differing levels of privacy. The high rollers sit in the VIP rooms on the upper floor, where they can look down, through the tinted windows, at their adoring subjects. They can see, but not be seen. I begin taking pictures, jotting down notes and measurements as I walk around. I'm getting more and more excited about this project. The ideas are bursting out of me. I can't wait to get home and start sketching.

Various workers are cleaning and prepping for tonight's crowd. I wonder if this is the same crew who will work the night shift.

As I watch a group of men carry liquor boxes to a stock room, I see the most handsome man I think I've ever laid my eyes on. He's tall, about six feet three inches, with wavy black hair, and topaz-colored eyes. His muscles bulge as he carries one of the heavy boxes into the storage room. He emerges moments later, brushing some dust off his torn jeans, which fit ever so nicely on his slim waist. He's also wearing a dirty form-fitting t-shirt, showing off the definition of his muscles, which I'm sure he works hard for. There's a dark smudge on his chin, and I have this overwhelming desire to wipe it away for him.

Now he's standing by the bar, wiping the sweat off his face—damn, he notices me watching him. If he'd given me a few more minutes, he probably would've caught me drooling too. I swallow and turn around, as if I'm busy doing something. I'm here to work, after all. I walk around the room again, trying to find the way up to the VIP rooms.

Ever have that feeling someone is watching you? That feeling that makes the hairs on the back of your neck stand on end? I have that very feeling now, and it's some strange magnetic pull toward *him*. I don't have to look to know he's walking toward me. I want to turn around, but I know if I do, I can't be held responsible for any inappropriate actions. So, I decide to ignore his approach.

"You need help?" he asks in a luscious baritone voice. I clench my legs as his voice reaches me in places that haven't been touched in months, if ever.

I turn slightly to look at him, hoping my face doesn't give me away. "Uh, yes. I was searching for the way to the VIP rooms."

My eyes linger on his pecs hidden behind the tight tee. Slowly I work my gaze down to his jeans where I try to imagine what type of action he is packing behind that zipper.

"I do have a face you know." He folds his arms across his broad chest.

My eyes snap up to his amused ones and I'm positive I've turned fifty shades of red.

"You must be the new interior designer."

"Yes." I clear my throat. "Yes, I am," I manage to stammer out.

He turns and walks away, and my gaze is firmly planted on his rock-hard ass. He stops and calls out, "Coming?"

I wish I was, preferably with him over me, inside me. I fall into step behind him as we walk to a hidden elevator. No wonder I couldn't figure it out. He swipes a card and the elevator doors open. We step inside the small space and I can smell an aroma of musk and man. There really isn't anything better than the scent of a man. I mean, a *real* man. He definitely has that scent on him, and he wears it well. Can I grab him by the collar and inhale?

The elevator stops and we exit, make a few turns down long, mirror-lined corridors and, voilà, we're at the VIP rooms. He leads me into a room with a dark blue and mahogany theme. I walk around, snapping pictures, as he lingers in the back.

"What's your idea for this room?" he asks, leaning against the wall.

"Umm, I don't know yet. I need to see the rest of the rooms. Then I'll let each room speak to me," I say absentmindedly, too caught up in my work to pay much attention to what my mouth is saying.

"How do you like the current theme?"

"I like it. It's dark, but I like it. Do you know who designed it?" I stop what I'm doing to turn and look at him.

He laughs at me; his lopsided grin looks much too good on lips that are much too kissable. I have no idea why he laughed at me, but I guess I said something funny. "Some French guy. Don't remember his name," he says, shrugging wide, well-built shoulders.

"You've been working for Pulse long?" Not sure why I'm asking him so many questions, but I love the sound of his voice. It does things to me.

"Since the day it opened," he says, still grinning at me.

"So, I guess, since you're still around, it's a good place to work." The club has been open for five years, opening several other locations since.

"You can say that," he answers. I look at him, noting amusement in his eyes.

"What do you do here? What's your role?" I'm curious if they keep him around as eye candy. Hell, I would pay big bucks for him to come to my office just to be my *personal* eye candy.

"I do various jobs. A little of this, a little of that." He pushes his hands into his pockets, his gaze never leaving mine.

Yep, he must be the eye candy. "Oh." His stare is so intense, other words get trapped in my throat.

He pushes away from the wall and turns to leave the room. I take it as an indication to follow him, where he leads me into another VIP room. This one is gold from high tin-tiled ceiling to plush carpets. It's rich and ridiculously elaborate. I repeat my routine of taking pictures, notes, and measurements. When we get to the fifth and last VIP room, I feel as if I need a cold shower. Not because of the work, but because of the pull I feel toward this man. His presence instantly commands a room, and it is most certainly commanding *me*. I fan myself with my notebook.

"Hot?" he asks, staring at me as if he's a lion and I'm his prey.

"A little," I say meekly as heat rises into my cheeks.

He heads behind the bar and fixes two drinks, offering me one. I taste it and smile. Jack and Coke. My favorite. He just might be my dream man.

"I take it you like Jack?" he asks, smirking at me again. I swear he makes me feel like I'm the butt of some private joke.

"Yes, actually I do. It's my drink of choice. My best friend constantly teases me about it." I don't know why I feel comfortable enough to share that with him.

"Well, it just means you have good taste. I like it when a woman drinks a real drink and none of that froufrou shit." He lifts his glass and I follow suit.

"Will your boss be okay with you drinking on the job?" I ask, genuinely concerned. I hate for his day drinking to rob Pulse patrons of all that lovely eye candy yumminess. If need be, I'll say it's my fault.

He shrugs and stares at me with his deep topaz eyes. "Sometimes you have to live dangerously."

"Well, here's to living dangerously." I raise my glass in another toast.

"To living dangerously." He clinks his glass to mine, his eyes boring into me. I feel like he's eating me alive.

"So you like danger, I take it?" Oh God, my flirtation is so obvious.

"It keeps things interesting. Makes for good conversation," he says, his leonine eyes darkening.

"That it does," I agree. I'm feeling quite dangerous right now.

"Afraid of danger?" he teases me.

"No," I lie, fighting the urge to pull on my collar to let out a little of the heat that's been building.

He raises his brow in a knowing look and says, "You should live a little. Try something dangerous just once. It's addicting."

"So, you're a thrill junkie?" If I were a betting person, I'd put all of my money on it.

"Yes. You never know what'll happen from day to day. Take life by the balls and enjoy it."

"Living life to its fullest," I muse.

Without me realizing it, my tongue caresses my lips, desperate for this man. His eyes darken further, intense. Hot. "Abso-fucking-lutely."

I swallow loudly. Why do I feel like we're talking about more than just living life to its fullest? "Umm...I have a boyfriend," I blurt out the words without thinking. Call it a defense mechanism.

He laughs an all-out, throaty laugh, throwing his head back and clutching his stomach, which I'm almost positive is an eight pack. If he would just lift his shirt up a little, I could confirm.

"I don't recall asking you, but that's good to know." He winks at me. Cocky bastard. He knows I'm attracted to him.

"I just thought I'd put it out there," I say. If I wasn't blushing before, I'm almost positive I am now. My cheeks are burning.

"And if I said I don't care you have a boyfriend?" The question lingers in the air around us. He waits patiently for my answer. Problem is, I don't have one. I've only ever been with one man.

I turn with my glass in hand and walk around the room. I feel his gaze on me and fan myself again. Damn Iggy for letting me get this pent-up with sexual tension. Feeling the other man close behind me, I stare out the tinted windows, looking down at the dance floor. I spin on my heel and find him mere inches from me. I take slow steps backward until my back hits the glass. No running from this. This is exactly what I was trying to avoid on the bottom floor where we first met. But right now, I'm more curious than ever to see what develops.

He leans in, ever so slightly, and my breath catches in anticipation. His lips graze my earlobe. He takes it between his teeth, tugging lightly. I gasp. I feel like such a slut; I don't even know his name. But honestly, if he offered me hot sex on a platter, I'd gladly say, "Yes, please, make it a double helping." Drawing back, he leaves me wanting more, and I'm suddenly aware of my heart banging against my chest and warmth flooding my body. I feel breathless but energized. I give him a questioning look.

"Bad timing, Tick." He turns away from me and talks to the man that let me in earlier.

How long has Tick been standing there?

Tick laughs out loud as I bow my head in horror, my cheeks on fire.

"Hmm, I'd say it was perfect timing. Miss Scott, I see you've found Tony."

Umm, did he just say…Tony? As in, Tony Delaney, the owner of the club? Chelsea's words from yesterday, *"Don't fuck it up,"* echo through what must be my empty brain. How the hell did I allow my hormones to put my career in jeopardy?

"Yeah, she found me. Take Manny and handle that business we were talking about earlier."

Tick gives me one last look before nodding and turning around to leave.

Tony stares at the door for what seems like an eternity. I rub my fingertips on the jewels of my necklace, wanting to scream or run. I haven't made up my mind yet.

"You're Tony Delaney?" I shift uneasily on my feet.

He turns around slowly and looks at me. The sexual energy gone, the charm leaving the moment Tick went out the door. "Yep. Looks like you're Anaya Scott." He turns and walks towards the door. I grab my things and follow him wordlessly.

We turn a few corners and arrive at a door. He swipes a key card, and a beep and a click sound before he opens it. He doesn't bother holding it open for me so I step in before the door slams shut in my face.

The office is large, with a glass and metal desk and large dark leather chair, and a couch on the other end with a coffee table. Behind the desk is a huge glass window that appears to have a full view of the club below.

He takes a seat behind the desk and powers up his laptop. I stand rocking back and forth in place, still holding all of my items. Is he not going to offer me a seat?

"May I have a seat?" My voice is snarky and I don't care to hide it.

Not bothering to acknowledge me, he keeps banging away at his keyboard. What happened to the hot alpha male from a few minutes ago? This guy is a fucking asshole!

I sit down in one of the chairs situated in front of his desk. I place some of my work items at my feet. *Okay, Anaya. Take control of this situation.*

"Mr. Delaney. Would you like to discuss the details of the project?"

"Hmm? Oh, yeah." He finally looks up and I'm reminded why I was lusting after this man in the beginning. "How long before you have some sketches for me to review?"

Sketches? I don't know what he is looking for in terms of design. "First, you need to tell me what sort of vision you have. Then, I can then come back with some workups for you."

He leans back in his chair, steepling his fingers. "Listen. I thought you had enough experience to handle this. If you don't, I can call Chelsea and ask for someone else."

Excuse me? Is he fucking serious right now? Didn't he request me specifically? My nostrils flare as I try desperately to control my breathing. "Even an experienced designer, as you say, would need some guidance as to the look you are trying to achieve." *Asshole.*

"Listen. I don't have time for those types of details. Mock something up and I will approve or not approve." He stands and walks to the mini bar to pour himself a drink. This time, no offer to me.

"What kind of budget?" I ask through gritted teeth.

He shrugs. "If I like it, I'll pay for it. If I don't, then I won't."

I open my mouth to speak but he cuts me off. "Is that all? I do have a club to run, as you can see."

I glare at him, wishing my eyes emitted death beams from hell, striking him down. Quietly, I gather my belongings and rise. Lifting my chin and with a straightened back, I walk toward the door. But then I realize I don't know how to get out of this freaking maze. I turn back to ask him but he has already picked up his phone and started dialing a number. With a shake of my head, I open the door and try to figure my way out of this hellhole.

## Chapter 4
### Howlin' For You ~ The Black Keys

I walk into C.F. Interior Designs an hour after my disastrous meeting with Tony Delaney, expecting to be fired. Instead of my usual hellos to everyone, I walk to my office with my head hanging low and my tail between my legs. I throw my items onto the client table and flop in the chair.

Banging my head on the table a few times, I fight back tears. What the fuck have I done? First, I shamelessly flirt with a person I thought was an employee for Pulse but turned out to be the asshole owner. An asshole owner that is sex on two legs. *God, Anaya get a fucking grip.*

I stand with a heavy heart and walk over to the window, wishing I could jump. But the window doesn't open and I'm afraid of heights. Go figure, it would be my luck.

Loud voices waft into my office and there's some kind of commotion in the main work area. I decide I should be nosy and see what the fuss is all about.

A bunch of the designers stand around Fran's desk. Her desk is covered with six large vases of long-stemmed pink roses.

"Oh my God. Those are expensive," Kelly, one of the designers, says as she places her nose against a rose, inhaling deeply.

"Fran, your boyfriend is a real sweetheart," I say, as I try to remember the last time Iggy has bought me flowers. Hmm. He never has. How have I not noticed that before?

"Oh, Sven couldn't afford something like this." She smiles.

"Fran, you little vixen. Are you stepping out on Sven?" I nudge her shoulder playfully.

"Oh gosh, no." She blushes. "I mean, they aren't mine. These flowers are for you."

I stare at her incredulously. Could Iggy be sending this as way of an apology? My skin tingles at the thought.

"Anaya, read the card." Fran hands me the sealed envelope with no signature on the front.

I never discuss my relationship issues with my co-workers. Most of them are happily married or happily dating, so why drag them into my drama. I usually make up bullshit stories about Iggy and I. Finally, a story I won't have to make up. I open the envelope with relish, and pull the card out.

*"Please accept this as my humble apology. I treated you badly, and you deserved better. The scent of these roses reminds me of you."* I read out loud to my adoring crowd, but choke when I see the signature. Tony Delaney. I recover quickly and say Iggy's name out loud. The girls crowd around me and tell me how lucky I am to have such an attentive boyfriend.

A bitter smile stretches across my lips as my stomach muscles clench.

"I'll help you carry these into your office." Fran stands and lifts a vase while I grab another. Three trips later, all six vases are decorating my small office. I sit and stare at them, unable to figure this out. He could've just emailed me an apology. This must have cost him several hundred dollars.

"Anaya, Tony Delaney is on line one," Fran announces on the intercom.

I grab the phone so quickly I chip a nail. "Mr. Delaney."

"Thought we were past that. We really should be on a first name basis, especially since I had a part of you in my mouth." His voice dances on the edge of humor.

A flashback from a few hours ago in the VIP room goes through my head and I clench my legs tighter. Catching my breath and coming back to reality, I hold the phone in a death grip. "The flowers are a little over the top, don't you think?" I whisper, even though my door is closed.

"What? Don't you like the way I apologize?" There he goes again, laughing as if I'm the butt of his joke.

"Mr. De-"

"Tony."

"Fine. Tony. I don't think you should be sending me flowers. I work for you."

"So it's okay for me to have my mouth on you, but it's not okay to send you flowers?"

Shit, when he says it like that, it sounds all kinds of wrong. Asshole. "You know what I meant."

"Actually, I don't."

I hear car horns honking in the background on his end, and it's making it hard for me to concentrate. Or is it his voice? I place my head in the palm of my hand.

"You're jumbling everything up." Thank goodness I'm sitting because my legs feel weak.

"What's that? Your voice is muffled."

I lift my head and clear my throat. "I said, you're jumbling everything up. You're hot and then you're cold. I don't get you."

He chuckles into the phone, that same throaty laugh I remember from when we were alone together. "Oh, you get me. And you want me."

I let out a loud guffaw. "Like hell I do." *Oh, yes I do. Very much so.*

"Angel, deny all you want, but you do." His voice is serious and confident.

What the hell did he just call me? "I'm not your angel."

"Ah-huh. I've gotta run. Bring a friend to the club this Friday night. You'll get the full VIP treatment."

I stare at the phone momentarily and place it back to my ear.

"And Angel," he practically purrs.

"Yes?" I croak as my belly does a flip-flop.

"When I say a *friend*, I mean, leave the boyfriend at home." And with that, he hangs up.

Well I'll be damned if *that* didn't make my panties wet.

## Chapter 5

**Bang and Blame ~ R.E.M.**

Ugh! I tear yet another page out of my sketchbook and toss it on the floor of my home office. I've been working on the sketches for Pulse over the last two days but can't seem to concentrate. My mind keeps drifting back to Tony Delaney, the roses, and our telephone conversation.

Rheda has been bugging me all day about what I am wearing to the club tomorrow night. One thing is for sure, I'm not dressing to impress him. I look heavenward to make sure lightning doesn't come down to strike me, because I'm such a liar.

I put my pencil to paper, again, to sketch something else. Unfortunately, my ideas just aren't coming out the way I have them pictured in my head. It's the equivalent of writer's block, I guess. But I can't afford to have "designer's block" right now, especially with my tight schedule. This project means too much to my career.

A drink, that's what I need. Maybe it'll help settle all this damn bubbling sexual frustration. I fix myself a Jack and Coke with a squeeze of lime. The first sip instantly relaxes me. I stand by the window and close my eyes, allowing myself to drift into a daydream. Fine ass, gorgeous smile, sinful earlobe play. For a minute, I think I can smell him. Heat rises up my neck and face, and I lay my head against the cool window glass.

"Anaya, you home?" Ignacio calls out. I can't help wishing it was Tony's voice calling my name.

"In my office," I answer, taking a seat at my desk and staring at the sketches scattered all over the place. I take a slow, measured sip, letting the whiskey do its thing—calm my frayed nerves.

"I knew I would find you." Iggy slurs his words, clearly drunk. Why's he home? He staggers over to me and gives me a sloppy kiss on my mouth. When he turns his back, I wipe away his vodka-flavored spit.

"You're home early," I say, mildly annoyed.

"Yeah. I was missing you, baby." *Missing me? Did I hear that correctly?*

"Is that so?" I remark, not really caring.

"Yeah. I wanted to come home to my beautiful girl." He staggers over to the bar and begins the difficult process of pouring himself a drink while hammered.

I stand up to help him, to avoid him making a mess. "Here, let me do that for you." I take the bottle from his hand and pour. I add a splash of soda and hand it over.

He smiles at me before taking a sip from the drink he really doesn't need, and staggers his way to my desk. "Whatcha working on?"

"Some sketches for a club."

"Oh," he says, accidentally spilling some of his drink onto the sketches.

I run over them with a napkin, trying not to scream. "Sorry," he mumbles, stumbling to my couch and plopping down, spilling more of his drink on my expensive white leather.

I blot at the booze coating my sketches as best I can. Those weren't even the better drawings, so I guess it doesn't matter, but I'm still annoyed with him. "Iggy, why don't you go to bed?"

"Hmm?" He looks up at me from the couch.

"Bed, Iggy. Go to bed." I can't help the edge of frustration in my voice.

He tries to give me a sexy grin, tilting his upper lip and showing his perfect, white teeth. He can't pull it off, though, since he's half in the bottle. "Bed, yes, let's go to bed." He makes an attempt to stand, but fails. On the second attempt, he succeeds. He stumbles over to me and tries to kiss me. Another woman's scent hits my nose, and I turn away from him in disgust. "Come on. Let's go to bed," he purrs, his voice a combination of drunken slurs and played out Romeo.

He's nothing like Tony Delaney. I fight the urge to sneer at him and his attempts to woo me. Too little, too late Iggy.

"No, *you* need to go to bed." I push him toward my office door. "I'm still working."

"Work! Work! Work! That's all you do, Anaya. I want to fuck. Now." He grabs my hands and tries to pull me into him. I manage to jerk away and put my two-thousand-dollar glass and mahogany desk between us.

"Iggy, you haven't even *thought* about touching me for *months*. Why now?" I'm truly baffled. He's been with a different woman every night, as far as I know. *Why is he suddenly aching for Anaya?*

It felt like a set up.

"I need an excuse to be with my girlfriend?" He scoffs at me, his bloodshot eyes roving over me warily, as if *he* should be suspicious of *me*. He's such a dick.

"Yes, actually, you do. You haven't been interested lately. I figured you got tired of me; you certainly haven't paid much attention these past few months. So, you know what? No, you cannot *fuck* me tonight." I stare at him, waiting for a response.

"You know what? I don't need this shit! There is plenty of pussy out there." He throws up his hands and scowls at me.

"Fine, then go out there and get it!" I snap in frustration. Sexual frustration. Not that I want *him*. I want Tony. I want him so bad I can't even have a proper fight with Iggy.

Anger flashes in his eyes as he rushes toward me with his fist clenched. My heart bangs in my chest and my hands tremble. "You know, that's the problem. I'm the only man you've ever fucked. You don't have the experience I need."

"Fine, then perhaps I should start fucking other men!" I yell and instantly see my mistake. He jerks closer and I stumble backward into the wall. Terrified he might actually strike me, tears begin streaming down my cheeks. He closes the distance, his face only inches from mine. He places his hands on the wall behind me, one on each side of my head. I can smell the stench of vodka and sex on him, and I want to vomit.

"If I ever find out you fucked another man, I'll kill you. Do you understand?" He's growling at me, like he's some kind of mongrel dog pissed that someone is getting to close to his bone.

I stare at him in horror, unable to form words.

"I said, do you understand!" He roars the words so loud I fear my eardrums might burst. I can only nod, my movements restricted by the close proximity of his face. He punches the wall then walks out of my office, slamming the door behind him. He's gone only seconds before I collapse, my ass hitting the floor, my head hitting my knees, my heart hitting the pits of despair.

I stay there until morning. I don't know how or when, but I must've fallen asleep. I wake up to the sun shining in through my office window. I stand up, my body screaming at me for staying in one position, on the fucking floor, all night. But I don't care. I only care that I wasn't actually hurt. That Iggy didn't hit me.

I open my office door…*is he out there*? I'm scared and angry at the same time. How dare he threaten me? How dare he manhandle me like I'm nothing? In all the years we've been together, I've never seen Iggy get like that before. It scared the shit out of me.

Would he do it? Would he really kill me?

I never want to find out.

## Chapter 6

## A Little Less Conversation ~ Elvis Presley vs. JXL

It's Friday night, and Rheda and I are in a cab on our way to Pulse. I'm still shaken up by last night's argument with Ignacio. His level of violence truly shook me to the core. I don't know how to process my emotions surrounding it. He's not the same person I fell in love with as a teenager. He's different in so many ways. He used to talk to me about his dreams; dreams that included me. Now we can barely speak without arguing. His touch used to set me on fire, but now it sends cold shivers throughout my body. What happened to us and how did we get here? I want to turn tail and run home; forget about going to Pulse with Rheda. Forget about the man who lit me up just so Iggy could shut me down.

"Anaya! Are you listening to me?" Rheda barks.

"Hmm… What? You said something?" I ask, my thoughts on everything but my friend.

"Yes. We're here. Come on." She pulls on my arm and we slide from the car. "What's with you tonight? You've been out of it the whole ride here. You and Iggy have a fight?" Concern flickers across her face.

"What? Oh, no. He came home drunk and went to bed," I lie. Now I know why abused women lie and cover up their bruises. It's because they're partially embarrassed, and also to protect their men. Twisted, yes, but that's exactly how my mind is processing this at the moment.

She stares at me before giving me a hesitant nod and tilting her head in the club's direction. "Okay, girl, come on, let's party our asses off!"

I smile hesitantly her as I take in the scene. The line has to be about two blocks long. Tons of people are going to get turned away tonight. But not us. We stop only long

71

enough to tell the bouncer our names, then we bypass the line.

Another large, tattooed man escorts us into the building, through the mayhem of bodies dancing and pressing up against one another, right to our VIP table, complete with chilled champagne. Our server pops the cork and pours us each a glass. Rheda downs her drink instantly and pours herself another.

"So, are you going to tell me what's wrong or what?" Rheda peers at me over the rim of her nearly empty champagne glass.

"Nothing. My mind is drifting because I'm trying to nail down some ideas for the club, that's all," I lie again. If I were a religious person, I'd swear I was headed to Hell for all the lies I'm telling. Especially to Rheda. My best friend.

She cocks a knowing eyebrow at me, as if to call me on my shit. "It's about Iggy, isn't it?"

I'm about to lie to her again but she raises her hand to stop me, then shakes her head. "I know it is. And I also know you'll never admit it to me. Listen, just so you know what's going on—because I'm almost positive he hasn't said a word to you—someone took shots at him last night. We don't know who yet. Also, someone has been attacking his supply houses."

"H-he didn't tell me," I stammer. Unbelievable. The man nearly dies and doesn't bother to tell me. What am I to him, really? How can he not share something like that with me? Honestly, it hurts. It hurts to know I mean so little to him, especially after how long we've been together, how much of my life I've given him.

Rheda offers me a sad smile. "I had a feeling he didn't, but there it is in a nutshell, honey. He's old school.

He won't tell his woman about what he considers his failure as a leader. I'm not saying he's all hearts and roses, but it might explain why he's acting different."

I nod, understanding what she's saying, though not understanding Iggy's idiotic mindset.

"Come on, let's dance!" She stands, shaking her ass. Still not out of my own head and ready to cut loose, I shake my head. She waves as she heads to the dance floor, and is instantly swarmed by men. By her smile and glowing face, I know she's enjoying the attention. Not that I blame her.

That could be me. I could be letting go, having a blast. Letting men touch me, touching them, and letting everything else just fall away under the music, lights, and heat. But I can't.

As if I already didn't have enough to think about, Rheda throws Iggy's near-death into the mix. How am I supposed to feel about all this—everything—every damn thing that's happened over the last week alone? Someone took a shot at Iggy last night? He keeps everything about his business a secret. Sometimes I wonder if that's the reason we've drifted apart over the years. My heart breaks a little for what we've lost. I thought we were best friends, but maybe the depth of our relationship was all in my head. Maybe he never felt as deeply for me as I had for him.

As a teenager, with my bouncing around from home to home, he remained the one normal, constant thing in my life. Sometimes I look at him and wonder if he still loves me at all. I think, deep down inside, I know he doesn't. I'm just a possession to him. Something he owns, like a car or a pair of shoes. Do I want Iggy hurt? No, I don't. But I don't deserve the violence, the coldness, and infidelity.

I lift my glass of champagne and take a sip, looking around the crowded club as throngs of people pulse together to the music. Then I see *him* standing by the bar. I can't see his face, but I'd know that ass anywhere. Shifting on the smooth black leather seat, I cross my legs and contemplate if I should go over to him. Maybe he can help me forget my lonely existence in a loveless relationship, even if for a moment.

Taking a few more sips of my liquid courage, I stand and smooth down my turquoise silk mini dress that hugs all of my curves. Placing one foot in front of the other, an extra sway in my hips, I make my way to him. Trying to maneuver through the press of frolicking dancers, I now know what popcorn feels like bouncing around in the bag in the microwave.

Long gone are the ripped jeans and dirty t-shirt that he wore a few days ago. He's in a suit, an expensive one at that. He's still facing away from me, but I see his muscles flex, as if stiffening. *Does he know I'm here? Can he sense me?* He lifts his head from his drink. "Jack and Coke for the lady," he says to the bartender, not yet turning to see if I'm even there.

"How did you know I was behind you?" I ask, stunned. Is he some kind of sexy, well-dressed wizard?

He slowly turns to face me. Our eyes meet. At that moment, I feel *owned.* I'm scared, but willing. "You don't know?" he asks, raising a dark eyebrow.

"No, I don't. How did you know?"

He steps closer and I catch the scent of his cologne, coupled with his own crisp, clean aroma.

"It's how you sensed me near you that first day. You felt it then, and you feel it now." He steps back and leans against the bar, grabbing the drink he ordered for me. He offers it to me and I take it, gulping down a fortifying mouthful. This man could drive any woman to drink. Thankfully, I have more control than that.

I think.

"I don't know what you mean," I lie. More lies? Yup, headed straight to Hell.

He smirks at me. "Sure you don't." Again, he looks at me as if he's told a joke and I'm the dummy who doesn't know the punchline.

Uncomfortable, I look around, watching the dancers for a moment before turning back to him. "It seems I'm always catching you drinking on the job."

He shrugs. "Are you going to tell on me?" His eyes are swimming with mirth.

"If you keep the free booze coming my way, I won't tell if you don't," I tease right back.

"Did I get the color right?" he asks in between taking sips from his drink.

I scrunch my eyebrows together in confusion.

"The flowers. Did I get the color right?"

I giggle and look down at my feet before looking back up at him. "Oh, that. Yes. Yes, you did."

"Did you tell your boyfriend about them?" His grin is wide and his eyes twinkle.

Boyfriend? That's right, I do have one, don't I. My chin tilts down and I cough. "Umm. No. There was no reason to, actually. Iggy wouldn't care. Besides, you sent them as an apology for being an asshole earlier." I try to smile but it wavers. Iggy wouldn't care if a man sent me flowers. But he'd kill me if I fuck another man.

"Really? So, what you're saying is your boyfriend is cool with random men sending his woman flowers?"

There is one thing Tony Delaney is not, and that is random. There is nothing random about this hunk of a sexy specimen that stands before me.

He steps closer to me and dips his head to my ear. His warm breath coasts my neck and I shiver. "If you were my woman, I'd kill any man that sent you flowers. You see, that would be my job and my job alone. I'd hate any man that brought a smile to your face, because I wasn't the one who put it there. I'm a greedy bastard, and I'd want to own your heart, your body, your soul, and everything else about you."

Before I can even blink, he is back in his original position at the bar, staring at the dancing patrons as if he had no effect on me whatsoever. As if his words didn't just rock the fuck out of me and tilt my world on its axis.

His topaz eyes smolder with intensity, and I lick my lips nervously. He reaches out and brushes a tendril away from my face and I lean in toward him, hoping to prolong the briefest of touches. He locks me into his gaze and doesn't let go. My knees begin to wobble as goosebumps appear all over my skin. His warmth, coupled with my own, feels like we can set this building on fire. His look turns to lust and I feel my thong get wet with need. A slow lazy smile spreads across his face as he reaches into his pocket, pulls out a quarter, and holds it up to show me both sides of the coin. I stare at it, then to him in confusion.

"Call it," he declares out of nowhere.

"What? Call what?"

"Heads or tails, Angel?" He takes a step closer.

"What do I win?" I ask, swallowing hard.

He bends and inclines his head to my ear. "Pleasure. It's always pleasure with me." He steps back again with a bemused smile. "Ready?"

"But, what do I lose?" *Hopefully, it's my underwear.*

He wiggles his eyebrows. "Nothing at all. It's all about varying degrees of pleasure. Now, call it." He holds

81

the coin up and tosses it in the air. Catching it, he holds it on the counter, his hand hiding the coin from view. He stares at me, waiting for my reply.

"Tails. I call tails," I say, as I imagine myself ass up, face down, him pounding into me with long, deep strokes.

He smiles, lifting his hand. "Looks like it's heads." He takes my hand and leads me to the dance floor. I barely have enough time to set my drink on the bar.

"I won a dance?" I challenge. I was kind of hoping I won something more.

Pulling me into his solid body, he sways to the music, to his own personal rhythm, and I feel as if the world has stopped for this moment. "If you'd gotten tails, I would have fucked you in one of the offices. Since you lost the toss, you get this dance instead."

*Wait! What? Can I get a do-over?* "Oh," is all I manage to say as I try masking my disappointment.

He pulls me in tighter and I feel every inch of him and his movements. He's a smooth dancer, and his rhythm is easy to follow. He's controlling me and the situation, and I like it. If I had to compare him to an animal, he'd be a panther. Yeah, he's definitely a panther. Lithe, forceful, and sexy—with a hint of danger. Instinct tells me I should run and never look back, but something stronger, deeper, captures me. I couldn't run even if I wanted to.

His scent is seductive, and I inhale him like a drug, feeling high. I place my hands on his tapered waist and feel his muscles bunching and flexing through the material of his shirt. I close my eyes and picture a perfect V cut into his abs. I imagine myself tracing my tongue around the cuts of his eight pack. I want to lick all of him like a lollipop. And possibly, just maybe, take a bite. With my face pressed against his chest, I smile at my thoughts.

Oh, this man, he has me forgetting who I am and all about the dangerous man who lies in my bed on occasion. Reopening my eyes, I look up to see his dilated pupils aflame with passion. Does he want this as badly as I do? I see a fleeting pained expression on his face. He stops dancing and grabs my hand, pulling me off the dance floor. I miss the closeness of him and want to make him stop so I can fold myself back into his embrace. Lost in my thoughts, I pause. Sensing my hesitation, he turns and smiles.

"Don't worry. Come with me."

And I do. I follow him because I don't have a choice. It's not that he's taken it from me. No, not that at all. It's because I know he and I are inevitable, and I've decided to see it through. He leads me into a back corner, far from the maddening crowd, to a hidden door. He swipes his card through a digital lock and opens it, allowing me to step in first. It's a storage room.

I turn to ask him why we're in here but he grabs me and backs me against a rough brick wall, lifting me up. I wrap my legs around his waist and my arms around his neck, and he kisses me before I can get a word out. His kiss is dominating yet soft, fierce yet gentle, demanding yet playful. His strong arms hold firmly to my back and, every now and then, tugs at my dress. A dress I hope he takes— no, rips—off of me. I feel starved and I'm ready to devour this man. I feel his cock fighting to break free. I wiggle down to greet his hardening bulge, yearning for the friction. He moans into my mouth, releasing his hold on me. He presses my back flush against the wall and places his hands on either side of me. Slowly, he moves his hands down to my waist and pulls away, placing me back on the ground. His lips are stained with my lipstick and I want to muss him up a little more.

"I've wanted to do that since you walked in four days ago," he growls against my ear.

I shudder in response. "Why didn't you?" I ask, curious.

Smirking at me, as usual, he admits, "Looking for the right time, right place, I guess."

"Oh, really? So, right now, in the storage room, is the right time and place?" Who am I kidding? Anytime, anywhere would have been the right time and place. An alley, pumping gas, washing windows... I'm not picky.

"The right place and time is yours to choose." He bends down and kisses me again, and I want to melt into him. He pulls away from the kiss, staring at me with dark and ravenous eyes.

"Fuck me. Fuck me, now." Hold on. Did those words just come out of my mouth? Maybe he didn't hear me. His eyes flicker with amusement. Damn, he heard.

"Aggressive, aren't we? I like my women aggressive, in a way. Just as long as you remember that, in my bed, I control you and everything about you."

Yeah, I heard, "Blah, blah, blah." What about sex? I'll take it however I can get it at this point. On the floor, the wall, on my hands and knees...I'll beg if I have to. "So, is that a yes to sex?" I ask shyly, excitedly. Hell, I haven't been this eager about sex in years. And the last time it was because I'd just ordered the Indulgences gift bag from Jimmy Jane...bullet vibrator and all. Best forty dollars ever spent.

"That is a no to sex, for now. You did lose the coin toss, after all," he jokes, his deep chuckle rippling into the small space.

I lost? Hmm... Somehow, I feel like I won. "Oh, so you're anticipating there *will* be sex in the future?" I ask, only half-serious. Okay, I'm lying again. I'm completely serious.

"Yes, there will be, and lots of it. I have a feeling, once I get a full taste of you, I won't get enough. You respond beautifully, and it's driving me crazy. I want you. And a body like yours is begging to be fucked by someone like me." He grins wickedly and I melt. How am I not a puddle of quivering want right now?

I bat my eyelashes. "I'm an 'in the moment' kind of girl, you know? I may not be interested later." I hedge my bets, hoping I'll hit big.

"Nope. No dice. Come on, let's get out of here." He turns and opens the door to a visibly angry Tick, standing and waiting.

Tony grimaces before looking at me. "Go to your table. I'll catch up with you in a bit."

I open my mouth to protest but his eyes plead with me not to argue. I let out a huff and walk past them both with an extra swish to my butt, letting him know what he is missing.

Sitting at my booth, I see the two men in what looks like a heated conversation. I try to look away, feeling as though I'm invading his privacy, but I want to know more. I want to know everything about this man. Eventually, Tick storms off, leaving Tony standing by the door, rubbing his hands through his hair. His face looks like a storm cloud that threatens to turn into a tornado. Our eyes lock for a long moment. Should I go to him? Will he come to me?

He answers the questions for me when he turns and disappears into the crowd.

Damn! My heart drops, along with my libido. Disappointment seeps into me and I slump into my seat. Rheda appears, plopping herself down beside me.

"Whoa. This place is incredible," she says huskily, out of breath.

"You've been dancing all evening, when did you find the time to notice?" I snap.

She looks at me, amusement on her face. "Jealous, are we? Stop being a prude and find a dance partner."

*I did find one, but he's gone*, I shout in my head. "Listen, I'm ready to go. Are you coming?"

She sighs, eyeballing the dance floor. "Yeah, I guess I'm ready." She shrugs.

I shift in my seat and frown. I was a bitch to Rheda and now I'm making her cut her night short. "I'm sorry for snapping."

She shrugs again. "No worries. I'm kinda tired anyway, and I do have to stop by the office tomorrow."

"On a Saturday? Something with Iggy's business?"

"Oh no. I do have other clients, you know. Besides, it's just for an hour or two and then I have to prepare for court on Monday. So, an early night is a good idea."

We both stand up and walk to the exit. Looking up, I see Tony staring at me. His dark gaze feels like a promise... Pleasure, hot sex, and lots and lots of orgasms.

*I just hope I can handle him keeping all those promises*, I think as I follow Rheda out of the club and into the sultry summer night.

Chapter 7

**Closer ~ Nine Inch Nails**

Having lunch at one of New York's trendiest restaurants is like a tug-of-war. Even though we made reservations, we still have to wait thirty minutes for our table to become available. Once Rheda and I are finally seated, I snatch up my menu because I'm starved. Also I need to get back to my office and work on more sketches for the club.

"We should go back," Rheda announces from behind her menu.

"What? Go back to the office?" I ask, confused.

"No, back to the club. We should go again, this weekend."

I want to say yes immediately, but I've had time to think since my encounter with Tony, and I have come to a conclusion. I'm a faithful person. I can't cheat on Ignacio. It's going to be hard enough working in the club with him around and me a big bubble of sexual frustration. Besides, it's not just about me being faithful, I also have to consider my career. He is, after all, my client, and sleeping with him will just complicate things further.

I shake my head in response to Rheda's declaration, and she pouts at me.

"Why not? Didn't you have a good time?" She places her menu on the table.

"I did. It's just that I have a lot of work I need to do for this club project." I'm not ready to tell her about my storage room encounter, or any other encounters Tony and I have had, for that matter. I never even told her about the roses he sent.

"Yeah, I guess you're right. This project is more important. We can go back when you finish." She picks her menu back up and bites her bottom lip as she tries to make a decision for lunch.

Thankful that, for once, her lawyer's perception is off, I let out a silent breath of relief.

Switching the subject immediately, I ask, "I have some sketches for the redesign of your bedroom for you to review. If you have time after lunch, we can stop by my office and you can take a look."

"Oh, goody. I can't wait to see your ideas for my boudoir." She claps her hands together in an animated fashion.

The waiter finally arrives and Rheda orders a medium rare New York Strip with creamed spinach, and I order filet mignon, Oscar style, with fried zucchini sticks on the side.

"So, tell me about some of the changes you are thinking about doing to my bedroom." She lifts up her drink with her index finger pointing straight in the air like a lady who "does lunch" would do. A woman's loud giggle echoes throughout the crowded restaurant. I look up to see who is having such a great time and that's when I see *him*.

My chest tightens, as does my grip on the steak knife I am holding.

"What's the matter?" Rheda turns in the direction I am staring. "Oh my. Who is that?"

I'm too busy cursing under my breath, wishing I could disappear and not witness this. A woman with jet black hair wraps her arms around him as he whispers in her ear, and she giggles out loud again. *What the hell is so funny?* She brushes her hand lightly over his chest, and pulls him in for what might be a kiss, but I look away.

"Rheda, listen, I forgot that I have a meeting in a few minutes. I've gotta go." I grab my purse and reach for my wallet inside. Not bothering to count out the bills, I just throw what I'm sure is a few hundred on the table, and stand.

"Wh-what? But..."

"I really am sorry, but I have to rush." I bump into a waiter, accidentally knocking his tray, and everything comes crashing to the floor around me. Steaks, salads, and soups go flying across the floor in different directions. I'm too upset to notice that some of the soup has splashed onto my shoes.

A quiet hush comes over the restaurant as all eyes are now on me. Rheda stands next to me, mumbling an apology on my behalf, and we rush out of the establishment as if we stole something.

So much for a quick and easy exit. I didn't need to look to know he saw me. Outside, in the blistering heat that matches my anger, I try to hail a cab with a for-once-in-her-life speechless Rheda.

"Anaya, wait," Tony's voice comes from behind.

Rheda turns to look at him but I have more important things to do, like get the hell out of here. Where is a damn cab when you need one? In the movies, you can always get a cab quickly after an incident. Not in real life, though.

A firm hand grips my shoulder and I want to punch him. I spin around and scowl at him.

"I wanted to make sure you were okay. You seemed…" He looks away, then turns back to me. "You seemed upset."

"Not at all, Mr. Delaney. I just remembered I'm running late for a meeting, that's all."

His eyes widen before his face tightens. "Okay, Ms. Scott. I assume the meeting is about my club's designs, since that is the only project you should be working on."

Rheda's mouth drops open behind him, but I ignore her.

"Of course, Mr. Delaney. I should have something for you to see by next week." I roll my eyes in an exaggerated fashion.

"Good, *Ms. Scott*. I expect to see something by tomorrow."

My hands tighten in fists and I open my mouth to say something slick back to him, but Rheda interrupts when she stands next to me and places her hand on my arm. "Why, of course she'll have something for you tomorrow. She was just telling me about her design ideas. You are a lucky man to have such a talented designer."

Thank God for Rheda because I was sure to lose my job for saying something worthy of my firing and subsequent time in jail.

Tony and I scowl at each other as my eyes drift to the spot where another woman had her hands on him.

*If I was his woman.* Ha! If I was his, would he know to keep his hands off of other women? Or would he be like Iggy and fuck anything with a vagina?

My jaw hurts from clenching it too tightly. I move my mouth around to get sensation back in it. "You shouldn't keep your lunch date waiting, Mr. Delaney."

His brows knit together and then his face softens. "She's not my date. She's my-"

"What? Your accountant?" I stab at him with my words.

His mouth forms a thin line. "Something like that."

"Well, it's no business of mine. I really must go." I turn back to the business at hand, getting a cab in a city of eight million. Are they all hailing one at once? *For the love of God, can I get a cab please?*

"You're right. It is none of your business. I expect to hear from you tomorrow," he spits out angrily and walks away. I flinch at his words.

"What the hell is going on?" Rheda asks.

"He's my client. That's all." I lift my arm, again, as yet another cab passes me by.

"That sure didn't look like the type of discussion one has with a client." She turns me around to face her, narrowing her eyes at me. I look away, hoping to avoid her seeing through any bullshit I may spew. "Is there something going on with the two of you?"

I let out a guffaw. "Puh-leez. He could only wish." No, that would be me. Didn't I beg for it a few nights ago? Fuck, how can I be so stupid.

Folding her arms across her chest, her blouse opens slightly in the front. "I'm not sure why you feel the need to bullshit me, but I won't push the issue with you." I let out a breath, as she continues, "For now. I can tell you are worked up. I just want you to know that I am here when you are ready to talk. Okay?" Her green eyes are warm and sympathetic.

I nod, unable to say anything further. She turns around and sticks a hand out and a cab stops instantly.

Well, fuck me! I guess when you got it, you got it, and I, apparently, don't.

# Chapter 8
### How You Like Me Now ~ The Heavy

Well, my little outburst yesterday caused me an all-nighter, working on sketches for the club. I guess that teaches me that going off in a jealous rage over a man who is not my boyfriend is just not worth it. Wasn't it? Instead of getting work done, I paced the floor, hoping I didn't wear out my expensive rug.

I was able to come up with something to present to Tony today. There is so much at stake with this and I just can't seem to get my emotions under control. How is it possible for him to have such a hold on me in such a short period of time? I feel like a rubber band that is wound too tight and ready to snap.

Fluffing out the curls that fall around my shoulders, I look into the mirror to see the dark circles from the lack of sleep. Looks like this will be a heavy concealer day. My eyes, which are normally wide and bright, look droopy and red. I drag my feet to the bathroom to look in the medicine cabinet for some Visine, which, as my luck would go, is a year past the expiration date. I let out a moan and throw it in the trash, then splash some cold water on my face.

I choose an ivory-colored blouse and a slim black pencil skirt, with zebra-print pumps. I keep my jewelry at a minimum and my makeup at a maximum. I look in the mirror, giving myself the once over, and decide it will have to do. Grabbing my sketches and purse, I leave my penthouse to hail a cab.

"Good mawnin', Mrs. DeLuca." Fred beams at me when I step off the elevator.

"Good morning, Fred." With zero coffee in my system and lack of sleep, my salutation comes out lackluster.

"Late night?" he smiles as he holds the door for me.

"Not the kind you're thinking." I smile dryly at him.

"Guess you'll be missing Mr. DeLuca while he is away."

My mouth drops open, but I quickly close it. Away? Iggy went away? He came home last night, for once, and said something to me, but I can't recall what it was. I was too caught up in trying to nail down an idea for the club without crying over seeing Tony with another woman, when just days ago, his hands were all over me.

"Of course, I will."

A cab stops and he opens the cab door for me. "You just holler if you need me."

"Thank you, Fred. I will." I get in, and he closes the door behind me. Did Iggy tell me that he was going away? I wonder for how long. I bite my bottom lip, trying to remember.

"Where to?"

"Oh. I'm sorry. 26 West 12th Street."

"A little early to go clubbing, isn't it?"

"I'm redesigning the club. Have you been?"

"Nah. Can't afford that place. A lot of my customers go there at night."

He turns up the music, and that is the end of our conversation, thankfully.

Twenty minutes later, I'm paying my fare and stepping out of the cab. I buzz the bell at Pulse and wait. The door opens after a minute or two, and a tall handsome man with an unlit cigarette dangling from his mouth opens the door.

His eyes roams over my body and I shift uncomfortably. "I'm Anaya Scott. I have a meeting with Mr. Delaney."

His shoulders droop slightly. "Oh, and here I was thinking you were here to see me." His voice holds a hint of humor.

"Nope. Sorry. Not unless you can approve my sketches." I hold up my empty hand. I look down and I don't have my portfolio with me. *Oh my God!* I turn around and look down the street in search of the cab.

"Something wrong?" He steps outside and looks down the block. "Trouble?" His hand goes inside his jacket, and that is when I see a shoulder holster housing a shiny object that is, no doubt, a gun.

I stumble back and he catches me.

"Woah. You alright?"

"My sketches," I croak, because my mouth feels like the Sahara Desert.

"Cab or town car?"

I close my eyes momentarily. "Cab."

"Shit. You're fucked."

*I know. Thanks for saying it.* "What am I going to do?"

"Well, I don't know, umm, Anaya? Right?"

I nod.

"Just explain it to Tony. He'll understand. He's cool."

Oh, no, he won't understand. Not the way I acted like a jealous girlfriend yesterday. My stomach begins to roll around, doing flips likes it's a gymnast going for a goddamn gold medal.

"Come on. Let's get back inside." I follow him with heavy feet.

How am I going to explain this? Visions of my career flying out of the window dance before my eyes.

He swipes his key card and the hidden elevator opens. "Ladies first."

I walk in, slowly, as I fight back the dizziness hitting me. When we get off the elevator, we hear raised voices that get louder as we walk closer to his office. His door is closed, but I can hear the shouting.

"Just wait here. I'll go in and tell him you're here." He smiles at me and I want to tell him never mind. If Tony is in a bad mood already, I don't want to tell him I lost the drawings. But it's too late; he opens the door and closes it behind him.

Whoever Tony is arguing with doesn't stop what he is saying. "Get your fucking head out of her pussy and back in the game."

"My head is in the game."

"The fuck it is. Listen, I'm your boy, and I'll call it the way I see it. You need to focus and stop sweating a piece of ass."

"She's not just a piece of ass."

A loud crash startles me and I let out a yelp.

So, he is daydreaming about the woman he had lunch with? What was I thinking before? That just because we kissed and flirted, he was mine? My palms feel clammy as a cold sweat forms over my body.

"Anaya is here. She's outside your office door. So, do the two of you want to tone down this shit?"

"She's here?" Tony asks.

"Yeah. Want me to tell her to come back so the two of you can duke it out?"

"I'm leaving." The door flies open, hitting the wall inside the office. Tick steps out and stares at me. His lips are pursed as he mutters something indecipherable under his breath and walks past me.

The person who brought me upstairs walks out next. He smiles at me. "He's all yours. I'm Manny, by the way."

"Thanks, Manny."

He nods at me and catches up to Tick. I stare at the two men as they turn the corner.

"You here to see me or them?"

My heart catches in my throat and I turn to face him. "You, I guess."

Tony gestures for me to come in. "Close the door and let's get this over with." He takes a seat behind his desk.

I try not to pay attention to the broken glass on the floor.

"Mr. Delaney." I pause for a moment to find the right words. "I want to apologize for yesterday."

His hand dismisses my comment. "It's nothing."

*Well, that was easier than I thought.* "I also must apologize for now as well."

This catches his attention as he jerks his head up. "Listen, don't –"

"I accidentally left the sketches in the cab a few minutes ago, and I'm so terribly embarrassed. If you like, I can quickly sketch out the basis of my ideas for you, and explain in detail."

He lets out a breath and closes his eyes for a moment. "It's okay." He opens his eyes again, then shuffles a few papers on his desk. "Listen. I've realized that my schedule doesn't really permit me to work very closely with you on the redesign. You'll have to work with Tick instead. He has my full authority on everything."

What? Work with Tick? What the hell just happened? "But-"

"If you'll excuse me, I'm really busy. You can see yourself out." He starts pounding away at his laptop as if he is going a few rounds with Mike Tyson.

I stare at him as I feel the walls closing in around me. "Sure. Goodbye."

I think I hear him mutter a bye but I am not sure because my head is officially spinning when I step out of his office. I let out a heavy sigh when the door closes. Shoulders slumped and tail between my legs, I walk down the hall and around the corner. The elevator door opens and Manny is about to step off with—guess what?—my sketches in his hand.

"Looks like we do have some honest cab drivers around." He hands me my portfolio.

I take it but my heart is heavy like the object in my hand. Perhaps Tony hasn't forgiven me for yesterday like he said. When will I learn to keep my big fat mouth shut? "Thanks," I mumble.

"Meeting over?" He tilts his head.

"Yes. He wants me to work with Tick instead." I feel hollow as I get on the elevator and Manny presses the down button.

"Is that so?"

I nod.

"Well. Tick is downstairs. Want me to take you to him?"

"Umm, no." I swallow hard and rest my head on the wall.

"Okay. He got your info?"

"I'm sure Tony will give it to him."

We both walk out of the elevator and he escorts me to the front door.

"Tell Tick I'll be in touch tomorrow," I say as he opens the door for me.

Once outside, I look at the time and realize that it's a little after noon. Perfect time for a cocktail to end this shitty day.

## Chapter 9
### Give It to Me Right ~ Melanie Fiona

Another sleepless night, but this time, it was anger-fueled and it came out in my designs for the club. I naturally scrapped the sketches that had medieval torture devices as backdrops, since I have a feeling Tick wouldn't be amused.

What the hell is Tony's problem? One day, he is all over me and the next, he is practically making out with another woman in a crowded restaurant. A woman who apparently walks around with Tony's face in her pussy. That burns me even more and I begin to reconsider reintroducing the torture devices to the designs again.

The only thing that is right this morning is that Iggy is still away, God knows where, and I can honestly say I could care less.

I get off the elevator at C.F. Interior Designs and say good morning to everyone, even though that is the furthest from how I'm feeling. Fran is running across the office, waving frantically as I am opening my office door. *I wonder what's wrong with her?*

A heavy, raspy voice speaks from behind my desk. "Nice of you to show up."

I yelp, jumping back and dropping my coffee, purse, and portfolio to the ground.

"I was trying to tell you that a person named Tick is in your office." Fran bends down to help me pick up my burdens.

"Here, let me help you with that." The large man is by our side and scoops everything up quickly, carrying it into my office and placing it on my desk.

"Wh-what are you doing here?" I finally manage to say as I feel my ears burn.

"I'll clean up the mess," Fran whispers. Why is she whispering?

She gives the large man a hesitant look and doesn't bother to wait for my response before she closes the door.

"Didn't Tony tell you that we are working together?"

"Y-yes. But I thought…"

113

"Hey. No time like the present. Thought I would swing by and take a look at the designs so I can get on with my day." He walks over to the client desk and picks up a cup of Starbucks coffee and hands it to me. "See, I came bearing gifts."

My recently purchased coffee having been a victim to the laws of gravity, I instantly salivate at the cup of yummy goodness in his hand. I think this might be the beginning of a beautiful friendship, especially if he keeps supplying me with coffee before every meeting.

"Thanks. I just wasn't expecting you." I sniff the cup and take a sip of the liquid gold. Mmm, just the way I like it. Dark and sweet.

"Yeah, sorry about that. Didn't mean to startle you and shit." He shifts from one foot to the other.

"It's okay. Have a seat and let's talk shop."

He sits his large frame in the small swivel chair by the client table. When I decorated my office six months ago, I did not have in mind that I would be entertaining someone of his stature.

"Alright, show me what you got." He leans back and takes his own cup of coffee in hand.

I reach for my portfolio and unzip the leather case. Opening it, I place it in front of him so he can flip through it freely.

He is silent as he looks through the designs that I have poured my heart, and some anger, into. I bounce on my feet as I wait for him to say something—*anything*. But he is silent as he examines each design. Every now and then, I hear "Hmm" or "Mmm," but that is it. My nerves are on end.

"Let me know if you have any questions." My voice sounds sing-songy but, again, he doesn't say a word.

My mouth feels dry, so I take a sip of my coffee and accidentally spill some on my pants. Fuck. Fuck-fuckety-fuck. I grab a napkin and blot at the brown liquid, thankful that I am wearing black pants today. I'll smell like stale coffee, but at least I won't have a stain that shows. That's something, I guess.

Closing the book, he looks up. I try to read his expression, but can't. "Damn."

*Damn? Is that a good damn or a bad damn?* If it's a bad damn, then I guess I might as well start packing my things, because Chelsea will be throwing me out before the end of the morning.

"You're fucking good."

"What?" My voice sounds like a squeak. I clear my throat. "Really? You like it?"

"Hell yeah. I'm not gonna bullshit you and say I understand all that shit, but fuck, it looks good to me."

"Do you need me to explain anything to you?"

"Explain? Nah. I'm good. When can work begin?"

"B-but those aren't really my better designs. I still have more sketches to do."

"Yeah. I get that. But I see where it's going, so I think we're good. Can I take this with me to show Tony?"

My moment's elation turns into a frown. I was hoping I would get a chance to show Tony myself. "Yes, of course you can."

"You need Tony to sign a contract?"

"Umm, yes. When I finish the last design submission, we will quote you a price. Once that is agreed on, we'll send Tony a contract, and then work will begin."

"Sounds 'bout right. Take the contract to Winta Grace, she's expecting you. She'll review the contract before Tony signs off." He reaches into his pocket and hands me a business card with her office address and number.

"Okay, I should have final sketches later this week, so contracts can be reviewed next week."

"Not going to work. Tony is looking to move forward with this. Have the contracts tomorrow. We can get the final designs later."

It's unusual for a client to work this way. "Is there a reason for the rush?"

He stands and walks towards the door with the portfolio in hand. "Nah. Tony just hates loose ends." He closes the door silently behind him.

I sit there, my mouth agape, but realize I didn't ask for his number. *God Anaya, what is wrong with you.* I go to my desk and see that Tick has left me a parting note on my computer. He changed my screensaver to his cell phone number. Yeah, I think he and I will get along just fine.

Fran opens my door, not bothering to knock, as she normally would. "Oh my God. Now that is what I call a man."

"Is he? I didn't really notice." I kick my feet on top of my desk and laugh.

"Yeah right, you didn't notice. How did he like the designs?" She takes a seat in front of my desk.

"He loved them. He wants us to send over the contracts to their lawyer tomorrow." I make a mental note to send a text to Rheda later.

"Good. Chelsea is here and wants to see you."

My heart plummets to my stomach. "What was her mood like?"

Fran shrugs as we both stand and walk to the door. "You know how she is. It's hard to tell. But I'm sure if she was in a bad mood, this will make her happy. She loves making money."

This is true. I walk up the winding staircase to the adjoining floor where Chelsea's office is located. Her executive assistant, whose name escapes me because she loses one every few months, announces me and buzzes me into her office.

Chelsea's office is cold and sterile-looking, like her personality. There is glass, and a lot of sharp edges. The office is decorated in various shades of white with hints of silver. I can imagine her looking out her windows while drinking the tears of children as she counts her next million.

"There you are. I wanted an update on Pulse." She sits behind her glass desk, which is as long as a ten-person conference table.

I stand in front of her desk, since she hasn't offered me a seat. "Tick just approved the sketches. He wants the contract in their lawyer's hands by tomorrow."

She beams brightly, probably calculating how much she'll need to buy another Porsche. "Well, Anaya. You surprised me. I didn't think you could handle this project, but I guess you've proved me wrong."

I grit my teeth at her backhanded compliment. "Thank you?"

"You're welcome. I will have the contracts drawn up and you can give accounting what you estimate to be the final costs. Make sure you hand deliver to his lawyer yourself."

"I will. I'll call and setup an appointment for tomorrow afternoon."

Chelsea has already picked up her cell and is typing out a message. I take that as my indication that I've been dismissed and leave. Once out of her sight, I do a happy dance for landing this account and not fucking up. Her secretary stares at me for a moment before shaking her head and going back to typing on her computer.

My future's so bright, I'm going to need shades.

## Chapter 10
### The First Night ~ Monica

With Pulse's contract safely in my briefcase, I wait inside the lobby of Winta Grace's law firm. The coffee table has old copies of *Architecture Digest* and *GQ* fanned out across it. I opt for flipping through the pages of *GQ*, since I already live the life that is pictured in *Architecture Digest*. Let's face it, what red-blooded woman doesn't want to ogle some hot men?

Faint sounds of coughing and printers echo from offices down the long hall. I cross my legs and settle into my uncomfortable chair. Clearly this wasn't designed for people to wait more than an hour. I look up at the polished receptionist who has been answering calls constantly. The floral arrangements decorating the space give off a scent of an English country garden.

Footsteps coming closer distract me enough to look up briefly, but then my attention goes back to looking at the sexy man posing in a Polo ad.

"Anaya?"

I'd know that deep baritone voice anywhere. My body, the horny bitch, betrays me and reacts to him.

Slowly, I close the magazine to see Tony Delaney standing in front of me with his piercing eyes.

"Mr. Delaney." My voice is curt and I don't care.

He crosses his arms over his chest, narrowing his eyes. "So, we're back to that?"

I place—hell no—actually, *slam* the magazine down on the coffee table, causing the receptionist to look up for the first time since I entered. I give her an apologetic look before turning a death glare at him. "Back? Didn't realize we ever left."

Most people would say my behavior towards him is not smart, especially since I technically work for him. But fuck him. Fuck him and the horse he rode in on. I'm tired of his hot and cold bullshit. He wants me but seems to be fucking another woman. Yeah, I know I'm a hypocrite but, at this moment, rationality has been tossed out in place of infuriation.

"Oh, Ms. Scott. I'm so sorry to have kept you waiting. I see that you've run into Tony. Our lunch date went a little longer than planned."

I turn to see the same woman who had her hands all over Tony at the restaurant. My mouth is agape as she stands before me with her hand out for me to shake.

With wobbly legs, I stand and take her hand, hoping she doesn't mind that mine is a little sweaty. Her straight black hair hangs just below her shoulders and her hazel eyes sparkle like jewels. Even in her expensive dress suit, she is sexy. You can tell she tries to downplay it when at the office. I bet if she played it up more, the jury would vote in her favor, all the time, hands down.

Tony bends and kisses Winta on the cheek, and I want to look away, but I can't. My heart feels like it's on a free-falling express elevator.

"I must go. I'll call you later about those plans we discussed." He turns to me and nods before taking his leave.

So, that's it? She gets a kiss and I get a nod? The bitch in me wants to blurt out that we did a little bit more than that a few days ago. But common sense takes over and I say nothing. My mouth forms a thin line as I try to keep secrets from jumping out.

"He is a sweetheart. I love that man." She smiles at me and points the way to her office. I follow behind her, occasionally glancing back toward the elevators.

Her office is decorated in dark mahogany wood, and rich jewel tones. It is almost masculine and not what I would have pictured for her. She takes a seat behind her large desk.

"You could've left the contract with Sheila. I hate that I kept you waiting so long."

I open my briefcase and hand her the object of our conversation. "It was fine. I didn't mind at all."

She opens the manila envelope and flips through the pages. "Hmm. It looks like Chelsea's standard contract. I'll have to go through it more closely, but I won't have time now."

Shit! Chelsea was expecting me to have the signed copies in hand when I went back to the office.

"Everything should be good to go," I try to nudge her.

"Oh, I'm sure it is. But Tony is still my client and I can't do a disservice to him by not reviewing this at length."

Nothing for me to add to that. I stand and lean over to shake her hand, when I get a glimpse of the picture frame on her desk. She notices me trying to get a better look at it and lifts it to show me, a bright smile spread across her olive skin.

"We were so young then."

Once again, my mouth is agape, like I'm trying to catch some damn flies, as I stare at a young Tony and Winta, holding each other and posing cheek to cheek.

My voice hitches before I'm finally able to say, "How old were the two of you?"

"Fifteen." She looks at the picture, tracing her fingers over their frozen faces.

*Fifteen? She's been with him that long?* Guilt hits me like a fucking wrecking ball. What kind of homewrecker am I? It's bad enough Iggy does it to me, but here I am, doing it to another woman? For once, I wish I was more religious so I could go to church and repent.

Are the walls suddenly closing in? Fuck, I feel like I'm suffocating. I grab my briefcase in a rush, stating, "You look like a beautiful couple."

"But-"

"I really must run. When you sign the contracts, I can have our messenger pick them up at your convenience. It was a pleasure meeting you." I haul ass out of her office and down the hall like the building is on fire.

Once again, the receptionist is looking at me like I belong in the insane asylum, and perhaps I do. I press the elevator and hope, for once in my life, something goes right. The doors open immediately and I thank a God I haven't prayed to in years.

Once the metal doors close, I press the smooth button for the ground floor, which should be labeled "Anaya's Great Escape." Leaning against the wall, I place one hand on the rail so I can hold myself upright.

I'm thankful for the elevator being empty but not for the crappy Kenny G. music that's playing.

How could Tony do that to her? Clearly, she loves him. You could almost feel the history they have together as she traced her fingers over the picture. Memories I'm jealous of her for. I want those memories to be of me and him, not the two of them. What is wrong with me?

The doors open and people give me room to walk off so they can enter. I want to knock them down, screaming, "Why her and not me?"

Once outside, the sounds of the city snap me back to reality. Why do I keep falling for men who cheat? Tony is just like Iggy, albeit a sexier version. He is still the same. A pedestrian shoulder checks me as he walks past me. Instinctively my hand goes to my shoulder to rub it. Another fucking asshole of a man. That's it, I've had my fill of it today. I'm going home. Chelsea can ream me out tomorrow.

I hail a cab and retreat to the safety of my home.

My penthouse feels empty when I walk in. Not because Iggy isn't here because, let's face it, he's never home. It feels empty of love. I decorated it in warm colors to make it feel like love but that's an emotion you just can't fake. I've tried to fake it all these years, failing miserably at it.

Sitting down on our custom-made couch, I kick off my shoes and tuck my feet underneath me. Looking around my living room, I realize what else is missing. Pictures. There are no pictures of Iggy and I together. None. We have pictures of old man DeLuca, Iggy's father. Some of Iggy alone or with friends, but none of us together. Geez, there are even pictures of Rheda and I together.

How have I not noticed this before? Like so many other things in my life I seem to overlook. It's as if, because I had a shitty childhood, I prefer to pretend that my adult life is perfect when it is so glaringly opposite.

I bet if I went to Winta's house, she would have pictures of her and Tony together all over. The walls, the tables, the desks, by her bed, or perhaps even in her wallet. A dull pain stabs at my heart and I choke back a sob. The only thing by my bed is a Kindle Fire. No pictures or illusion of love. Just the obvious; I'm lonely. I live with a man and I'm lonely.

Standing, I walk over to the wet bar and fix myself a much-needed drink.

I pour two fingers of Gentleman Jack and forego the soda. I gulp the amber liquid, enjoying the delicious burn as it goes down my throat. I pour another. *Anaya Scott, you deserve to get rip-roaring drunk today.* Perhaps it will help fill the emptiness in this house.

The doorman's telephone buzzes by the door, and I debate if I should answer it. I'm not expecting anyone. But then I remember I was expecting some swatches I ordered.

"Yes?"

"Mrs. DeLuca. A Tony Delaney is here to see you," Fred announces.

The phone slips from my grasp when I hear his name. *Tony?* Maybe my alcohol-induced brain heard that wrong.

"Mrs. DeLuca? Are you there?"

I hear Fred's worried voice over the phone, lying on the floor. I bend to pick it up and place it to my ear. "Sorry, Fred. I dropped the phone. Did I hear you correctly? Did you say Tony Delaney?"

"Yes, ma'am. Shall I send him up?"

*No. Absolutely not! You don't invite the devil into your house.* "Yes, please do." I hang up without saying bye. I'll have to apologize to Fred later. My mind has gone numb as I pace the floor in front of the door.

I hear the elevator arrive in the vestibule and I immediately open the door to see him walking out. Still in his dark navy Armani suit I saw him in earlier today at Winta's office. Winta, his longtime girlfriend! Anger hits me and I take my glass and throw it. Good thing for me, but mostly him, that I'm a terrible pitcher, especially when tipsy. I wasn't even close to hitting him.

He stares at the wall the two-hundred-dollar crystal glass has shattered against.

131

Amusement flickers in his eyes. Asshole! I'll show him. I turn in search of another glass; I've got a fully stocked bar, so I'm not without plenty of ammo.

"This is the way you normally greet your guests?"

I turn to scowl at him as I stumble my way across the living room and to the bar. *Ouch*! I stub my toe on a chair leg. *Oh, he's going to pay for that, too.*

"I don't remember inviting you." I hop on one foot, rubbing my toe. I'm pretty sure I look like a hot mess. Then something dawns on me. I stop hopping and turn around again to look at him. "How did you know my address?"

He looks down, avoiding eye contact with me. "Chelsea. Told her I needed to go over some design stuff with you." He flashes those gorgeous eyes at me and, for a moment, I forget that I'm mad at him.

"She had no right," my voice quavers.

"Don't blame her, I can be persuasive when I want to be." He shoves his hands in his pockets.

He doesn't need to remind me of the power of his persuasion. He's a walking billboard of it. Damn him.

"What do you want, Tony?"

There goes that damn smile again. One of these days, I'm going to ask him what's so funny. "You're not going to offer me a seat, or at least a drink?"

"Nope. You won't be staying that long. What do you want, so you can leave."

"I was hoping the two of us can call a ceasefire."

I bite my bottom lip as I mull this over, weighing the pros and cons. I need to try to get along with him for the sake of my career. But he just makes me so damn mad—madder than Iggy ever has, and that's saying something.

"Winta said you ran out of her office so I wanted to come over and talk to you."

And just like that, the ceasefire I was debating, has gone out the window. My nostrils flare and my fists clench together. He has a sweet girlfriend who was worried about me and he comes over here, *for what?* Fighting with him is the only thing that stops me from tearing his clothes off and riding him like a horse.

I spin on my heel, dead set on getting another glass to throw at him. He follows behind me as I grab another one. My grip is so tight, I fear it might shatter. Lifting my pitching arm, he stalks over to me, grabbing my arm and pulling me into him. He slams his mouth down onto mine. The faint stubble of his whiskers scratches my top lip, and it feels delicious. Glass forgotten, it falls out of my hand, hitting the ground as shards prickle the top of my bare feet. Tony lifts me in his arms without breaking our kiss. I wrap my legs around his slender waist, feeling his growing erection through the material of his pants. The desire to rub myself against him is almost unbearable.

The tastes of mint coupled with whiskey is sexier than one would ever think. I want to bottle this up for another time and break open—in case of an emergency.

His tongue explores my mouth as I savor his flavor and everything about him. My heart is beating so fast it feels like it's going to jump out of my chest and into his hands where it belongs. Because he owns it.

Reaching down with one hand, I try desperately to undo his pants but I'm unable to. Fuck! I need to feel him inside of me like I need goddamn air.

Because my skirt is hiked around my waist I'm startled at the instant cold hitting my ass when he gently places me on my glass desk. Suddenly, my ass cheeks feel cold as he places me gently on my glass desk. All thoughts of Winta and Iggy push out of my mind as he sweeps away the contents of my desk in one fluid motion. Sketches and pencils clatter to the floor. It turns me on more knowing he is as hungry for this as I am. I will deal with the guilt later, after he gives me an orgasm or two. Then I'll kick him out. I'll even say he's a shitty lover in bed, but I really, *really,* need this now.

He lifts my hips with one hand and grabs my Hanky Panky low rise thong with the other, slowly lowering it down my ass. He stops moving the delicate lace midway and kneels in front of me. Eye level with my sex, he rubs my inner thighs with his roughened fingers, flipping a switch inside of me.

My skin feels like it's on fire and it's a flame that only this man can put out. He moves his hands closer, ever so closer, to my warmth. The agony of it all is killing me and I want to take his hand and guide him home. Matter of fact, while I'd happily fuck his hand, I need another part of his anatomy to stoke this flame.

I lift my hand to place on top of his, but he shakes his head with a smirk. Memories of his words from the storage closet play out in my head: *"I like my women aggressive, in a way. Just as long as you remember that in my bed, I control you and everything about you."*

He reaches for my thong and gently tugs it past my knees and to my ankles. Again, he doesn't completely remove them and I want to shout, "What are you waiting for?" Instead, he lifts my foot and licks my right big toe teasingly. I let out a loud moan and his mouth completely engulfs it. His tongue swirls around my toe. His mouth is warm, and his tongue is tickling me. What a wonderful combination. Yet another thing that I want to bottle up and save for later.

I wonder, for a moment, if it is possible to have an orgasm from this alone, because I feel like I'm well on the way to having one, and soon.

"Oh, God." The words escape my mouth as my head falls back. My hair brushes against my shoulders, adding yet another layer of sensation.

The hum from his chuckle reverberates against my toe, still in his mouth. He releases me and I lift my head to beg for more. I open my mouth to protest but he moves to the crotch of my panties, where he inhales deeply. Oh. My. God.

I feel hypnotized by this man. Slowly he pulls my thong the rest of the way off and gives it one last lingering sniff before placing it in his pocket. What the hell; it's minor payment for the way he's making me feel.

He stands and places his hands on his belt. Now, this is a part that I want all to myself. I hop off of the desk and saunter in front of him. It's my turn to shake my head at him as I remove his hands from my job. I undo the buckle and unzip him.

Funny, I would've thought my hands would tremble, but my hands are steady and sure. Tony steps out of his shoes and kicks them to the side. He reaches into his pocket and pulls out a foil packet, before I lower his pants and boxer briefs. He kicks off his pants, one leg at a time, as I lower the straps of my dress, letting it fall to the floor.

Standing before him in just my hot pink bra, I press against his hard chest and massage his shaft in long strokes. I feel the veins of his dick throbbing in my hand. He places his hand over mine and pulls my hand up and down, much rougher than I was.

"You can't hurt me," he says into my ear, his warm breath reaching in and grabbing hold of my raging sex. I just nod into his chest, because basic words escape me.

Precum coats my fingertips and I realize I want to taste him before he enters me. I kneel before him, eye level with his erection. It's long, thick, hard and, if it is possible to call it beautiful, I would. Because it is, just like the rest of him.

My eyes bore into his, blazing back at me with lust and desire. Slowly I slide my mouth down his cock as far as I can take him. Humming my satisfaction of finally tasting him. He hisses out a breath and his hand flies to my head, fisting my hair. With one hand I work the base of his dick, while the other plays between my legs. My wetness coating my fingers as my fingers slide effortlessly, my nipples harden as my arousal heightens.

"Fuck. Angel. Now. I need you right now." His voice is ragged and I'm dazed.

I slowly, ever so slowly, pull my mouth and tongue up his shaft until I am at the tip. I suck deeply before removing my lips. He tears the foil of the condom as I stand up.

"Over the desk." He doesn't ask, he commands it, and I willingly obey.

I bend over the desk as instructed, my ass up and on full display. I feel him coming closer until our legs are touching. The course hair of his thighs rubs against my smooth ones. He nudges my legs with his knee gently, spreading my legs wider, and my breath hitches in anticipation. Tony reaches one hand in front of me and rubs my clit as I let out a loud moan. "I want to taste you. But it will have to wait," he murmurs.

He glides himself into my slick opening and I gasp. He stretches me, oh so wonderfully, and I feel my walls opening up for him. Taking him all the way in, he fills me completely to the point I think I can't take any more. Then he stills, and my heart seizes.

"Wh-what's wrong?"

"Nothing." His voice is strained. "You feel so fucking good."

I'm about to return the compliment when he grabs hold of my waist and begins to plunge into me. In and out, in a beautiful rhythm. He is the musician and my body is the instrument, and together we are making this perfect harmony.

My arousal builds and my breath quickens. Beads of sweat drop from my forehead onto the glass. My body tenses and I arch my neck. He reaches in front of me again and rubs my clit. My walls clamp down tighter on him as I scream out my climax.

My voice is hoarse and he is still giving me every part of himself. I want to scream again, but the words are lost in the series of moans. How can this be? I-I'm coming again. So soon? My arms splay across the table, fingers clutching at air, when he finds his own release. His grip on my hips are so tight I'm positive it will leave a mark. And I don't care. I want him to mark me, own me, control me. As long as it's *just me*.

And that's when Winta's face flashes in my mind, and guilt hits me, like all those dodge balls I missed in gym when I was in high school. I try to push up, but he is too heavy.

"Get off," I snap. My post-coital bliss is a distant memory as guilt has taken its place.

"What?" He stands, and I feel the emptiness when slides from my body.

I throb for him as my muscle walls contract, missing him. Ignoring what I want, I turn to face him. "That is never happening again."

His expression hardens. "What the fuck is wrong with you?"

"What the fuck is wrong with me? What's wrong with *you*?"

He removes the condom from his perfect cock, before reaching for his briefs and stepping into them. I want to kiss his dick goodbye. It does, after all, deserve a parting kiss, but I shake the image out of my head.

"Angel, don-"

"Don't you call me that. You don't have the right."

Now reaching for his pants, he steps in, one foot at a time, and pulls them up. "I was just inside of you. I think I have the right," he roars.

"Leave, Tony."

"Not until you tell me what the fuck is going on." He zips up his pants but leaves the belt hanging open.

"Oh, don't tell me you forgot about *her*. Your girlfriend!"

"Girlfriend?" His brows knit together and then he places his palm over his forehead. "Shit. Winta?"

"Yes. She showed me the picture of the two of you. I saw you at the restaurant. You're just like Iggy. You'll fuck anything, even when you have a good woman at home. Well, I'm sorry for what I just did to Winta, because she didn't deserve that."

"She's not—"

But I'm already too busy gathering my things and walking out of my office toward my bedroom to pay him much attention.

"You can see yourself out, Tony." I slam my bedroom door behind me. Leaning against the wall, I listen for him to leave. I wait a few more minutes before walking back into the living room to make sure he has, in fact, gone. I'm so confused about him leaving, me still wanting him, my betrayal of Winta. Every type of emotion goes through me but one. I don't feel guilty for what I've done to Iggy, not in the slightest. Guess that should mean something.

## Chapter 11

### Wicked Game ~ Emika

*"Fuck. Angel. Now. I need you right now."* The memory of Tony's words from last week hits me as I stare at an armoire in ABC Furniture Warehouse. Placing both hands on top of the polished wood, another memory hits. *"Over the desk."* My body reacts to his words, once again. I close my eyes and clench my legs together tightly, when another echo from the past comes. *"I want to taste you."* I lift my hair from the back of my neck and fan myself with my open hand.

One week. It's been a whole week since I laid eyes on him, had him inside me, and enjoyed every delicious inch of him. When I went to Pulse a few days later, to go over the project schedule with Tick, he informed me that Tony left for a last-minute business meeting at one of his other clubs. I foolishly fought back tears. Wasn't I the one who pushed him away?

"So, what do you think?" Rheda asks from behind me.

I'm startled for a moment; I forgot that she was with me. "About what?"

She rolls her eyes in an exaggerated fashion. "About the charity dinner. You'll be one of the participants, won't you? We need as many as we can get." She is referring to the Rape Victim Charity dinner she is hosting. Rheda is extremely passionate about rape victims, because her older sister, Haylee, never sought help after being raped, and eventually killed herself. Rheda swore she would do everything she could to make sure no other woman goes through what her sister went through. That's when she founded *Haylee's Survivors*. It was important to Rheda that victims of rape not feel alone in their struggle, that they know they aren't victims, but survivors.

*Participate in what? How long was she talking?* Ever since I kicked Tony out after the best sex of my life, I've been in a damn daze. Yet another thing I can blame him for. "Of course, I will. Anything you need," I readily agree, not quite sure what I've committed myself to. In a very rare act of emotion, she gives me a quick hug.

Back to business, she dabs at her eyes. "I knew I could count on you. Also, I need you to see if you can sell more tickets."

"Hmm. I think I might be able to get a few more people at the office to purchase tickets."

"Thanks. Any little bit helps." Rheda examines a pillow then throws it back into the pile. "How is the redesign of Pulse going?"

"It's going. I've been working with Tony's associate, Tick. He usually just nods and tells me 'go ahead and do your thing.'" I state as I look at an oak-framed bed.

"Well, that should be a good thing, right?"

"Yes, I guess." I'd much rather have my meeting with Tony, but the distance is what I need.

"Has Iggy figured out who's attacking his storehouses?" I ask, partly because I want to change the subject. I never told Rheda about what happened with me and Tony in my home office last week.

Shaking her head, Rheda answers, "Still nothing. It's like the person is a ghost. He knows the perfect times to hit. His team is extremely organized and fast. Ignacio thinks he may have a mole in the organization."

"A mole? Any ideas of who it might be?" Because Iggy keeps most of his business away from the house, I haven't met many of his men. I know a few names here and there, but not enough that I can help pinpoint a mole.

"He has his eyes on one or two of his men, but he hasn't shared the names with me."

"So, he's still in danger?" On some level, I'm concerned, and on another, I could care less.

"Your guess is as good as mine. All I know is that's the reason for his quick departure. He wanted to lay low for a while and regroup." She starts digging through her purse for something.

"When will he be back?" Clasping my hands together, I rock slightly, waiting for her answer.

She shrugs as she looks into her compact mirror. "I don't think he has a set date."

Pleased, I turn my head as a slow smile spreads across my face, and then, the thought hits me— "Am I in danger?" Why did I not consider my own safety in all this? I'm Iggy's girlfriend, could I be a target?

Snapping her mirror shut, she casually tosses it back in her purse. "No. We don't believe so. You know the Mafia code: no women or children are touched."

I let out a breath and a shiver goes through me, as if someone walked over my grave. Shaking off the feeling, I stroll to another bed, only glancing over it, all desire to pick furniture swept away with talk of Iggy.

"Is that you?" Rheda accuses.

"Huh?" I scrunch my eyebrows together in confusion.

"You. Your phone. Is that you?" She points at my purse.

Oh, shit. That *is* me. I open my Birkin and search through it until I find my cell. Not bothering to see who is calling, I answer immediately. "Hello?"

"Oh, hey. Wanted to let you know that I have to reschedule our meeting for tomorrow. Some shit came up that I gotta handle." Tick's voice comes over my phone.

"Sure, no problem. Just let me know when you would like to reschedule for."

"I gotta get back to you on that. But listen, go ahead and do your thing. I'm sure I'll like it."

Rheda is now standing in front of me, mouthing, *Who is it?* When I tell her, she replies, *Ask him to buy tickets.*

I shake my head at her as I try to pay attention to what Tick is saying. Rheda stomps one foot down and narrows her eyes. God, she can be annoying sometimes, especially if she doesn't get her way.

"Ugh, Tick. I don't normally ask my clients to do this…" I pause to glare at Rheda before turning my back to her, "…because it is probably *unethical*, but my best friend is chairperson of *Haylee's Survivors*, which is a rape victim charity. She is hosting a banquet in two weeks, and I wanted to know if you would like to purchase tickets for the dinner. It's two thousand dollars a plate."

"Yeah, sure. I'll purchase some. Give me the deets the next time I see you, and I'll write you a check."

"Thanks, Tick. This is greatly appreciated."

"Anything for charity. I'll talk to you later."

"Wait. Tick. Are you there?"

"Yeah. 'Sup?"

I look at Rheda out of the corner of my eye, her green eyes flickering with curiosity. "Tony. Is he back?"

He clears his throat. "Why?" His voice is guarded.

*Think, Anaya, think.* "Just wanted to know, in case I need him to sign off on anything."

He inhales. "Listen, Anaya. I like you. So I don't want you to take this the wrong way. Tony's got a lot of shit he's dealing with. He needs to be focused. You in the mix is not going to help. I'll tell him you asked about him cause I'm not the type of asshole that keeps shit from his friends. But I will say, I'd rather you stop asking for him." Tick, a man who rarely wastes times with little things like saying bye, hangs up the phone.

Rheda stares at me as I try to decipher what Tick meant. She opens her mouth to say something, but I shake my head, unable to answer any questions because my mouth feels like cotton.

# Chapter 12

## Your Woman ~ White Town

"Thanks, Manny, for helping me take down these measurements." I say, as I try to balance myself on a ladder on one foot while reaching out a hand to get the correct numbers.

"Yeah, sure, no problem. I'm all about helping the ladies," Manny says with his usual unlit cigarette dangling from his mouth.

"You know, smoking is bad for you."

"Walking across the street can be bad for you. Life in general is bad for you. My cigarette ain't going to hurt nothin'."

"Hey, dickhead. Did you take care of the liquor shipment?" Tick says, as he walks into the room with a clipboard in his hand.

Manny holds out his hand to help me step down from the ladder. "Didn't get here yet."

"Shit, Anaya. Didn't know you were here."

"Sorry, I just needed some more measurements. I didn't want to disturb you for that." I retract the measuring tape, avoiding eye contact with him because I'm still smarting from our conversation a few days ago.

"Yeah. Listen. Let me holla at you over here for a sec." He points his head toward the VIP booths.

Manny shrugs and walks off. I stare at Tick for a moment before walking in the direction of the booths, and he follows. I take a seat and wait for him to begin.

He shifts his large frame in the booth. "I'm not good at this shit. But I'm sorry for coming off a little rough the other day. I don't want you to get hurt and I need Tony to remain focused. He's juggling a lot and you were a surprise."

Juggling? I guess juggling the women in his life, or is he talking strictly business? "Well, I guess it can be difficult when you're juggling work and different women." *Oh, yes, I know I'm a hypocrite, and I don't care.*

Amusement flickers across his face. "Women?"

153

I open my mouth to tell him that I'm not naïve, but something catches my eye. Manny is going over what looks to be a liquor shipment with someone. I recognize the person he is talking to as Jay, one of Ignacio's men. Why would he be here?

Tick turns his head in the direction I'm staring. Before he gets a chance to say anything, I rise and walk in the direction of Jay and Manny.

"Jay?" I call out as I close the distance between us, forming a triangle with Tick bringing up the rear.

Jay blinks rapidly and smiles. "Oh, Anaya. Didn't know you were here. How's it going?"

"Fine. What are you doing here?" My voice is guarded, suspicion rising.

"He's here to deliver the booze." Tick nods at Manny, who ushers Jay in the opposite direction. Jay barely has enough time to say goodbye.

I spin around to look at Tick. "Do you know who Jay works for?"

"Yeah, he works for Ignacio DeLuca. Our liquor supplier."

This is too much of a coincidence. Or am I reading too much into this? My mind races, trying to calculate the odds.

"How do you know Jay? You buying bootleg booze?" He perks an eyebrow and smirks at me.

"Wh-what? Umm no. Of course not. I know Jay from…" I wrack my brain, trying to figure out a way to say how I know Jay, without saying his boss sleeps in my bed on occasion.

"Ehh, it doesn't matter. Listen, we have to be guarded about who knows about us buying illegal liquor. If you don't mind, I would prefer if you didn't say anything."

"Y-yes, of course. Not a word." I pretend to lock my mouth shut and throw away the key.

Tick turns to walk back toward the booths. "You coming?"

I turn to walk but I glance back over to Manny and Jay. Damn, what a coincidence.

# Chapter 13
**Dreams ~ Fleetwood Mac**

It's the night of the *Haylee's Survivors* charity
dinner at the Rainbow Room atop of Rockefeller
Center, on the 65th floor. I'm in a Ralph Lauren satin
crystal pink ball gown, with Swarovski jeweled ivory
color stilettos from Jimmy Choo. My hair is in an
upsweep with a few hairs curled delicately, hanging
loosely in the back. Rheda looks stunning in a dress that
matches her flaming red hair. Her ball gown
accentuates her curves and makes her B-cup breasts
look at least a size bigger. Her hair, which is naturally
wavy, is bone straight and radiant. She is wearing her
sister's favorite gold earrings; they spell out Haylee.

"Looks like this is a success," I say to Rheda as
I sip on my glass of champagne.

"Well, we will know better after the auction,"
she says absentmindedly, before seeing someone and
running off to greet them.

*Auction?* I've been such a damn space cadet
over the past few weeks I might've missed some add-on
that she mentioned for tonight. I look around the room

to see if I can spot the art she is auctioning off, so I know which pieces to bid on. But I see none. What I do see is Tick walking in with a very leggy brunette with ice blue eyes and an emerald green cocktail dress. Behind them, Manny walks in with—wait for it— twins! One on each arm. I shake my head at the sight.

Then I see Tony enter with Winta on his arm, and my heart stops. My legs feel weak and I turn, in search of my table. I need to sit before I fall over.

"Hey, baby girl." Tick stands behind me. "Walking off before hollering at a brotha?"

With most men his size, the suit would smooth out the rough edges of their attitude, but somehow, Tick is handsome yet intimidating in his tux.

"Oh, sorry. Didn't see you. Was trying to find my table," I mumble.

He winks at me. "Sure." He turns his head in Tony's direction. "Tony's here, in case you were wondering."

"Is he? I didn't notice." I look down at the floor, hoping it'll open up and swallow me whole.

"Yeah, he's into donating to charity, it seems."

"Well, anything for the cause. I really should find my table." I turn to leave, but he holds my elbow.

"Come on. Manny's here, too."

"Sure. Just for a sec."

He ushers me in their direction, and my eyes lock with Tony's. I want to look away but I can't. Desire, want, *need* pours through me, and mirrors in his eyes.

"Anaya, you look stunning. I'm so glad to see you." Winta walks over and gives me a hug.

Guilt slams into me…the way her boyfriend did a few weeks ago. The only difference being the guilt cuts like a knife in my heart.

"Winta, yes, I'm happy to see you as well." I give her a gentle squeeze.

Winta's dress is off-white, with black applique and a sweetheart neck. She isn't wearing jewelry; who needs it when you have Tony as an accessory.

"Anaya." Tony bends and kisses my cheek gently, a painful reminder of my betrayal of Winta. He lingers a moment too long. "Angel, I have to talk to you," he whispers in my ear.

A bitter smile spreads across my face. "When hell freezes over, Mr. Delaney." I step back. "If everyone will excuse me. I have to powder my nose." I give the age-old excuse that women always use to make a fast escape.

"I'll come with you. I need to freshen up my makeup," Winta says and links arms with me.

We find the ladies' room and the attendant greets us. We take a seat at the vanity, opening our purses.

"Tony speaks very highly of you," Winta says, in between applying her lipstick.

I wonder what he has told her. Perhaps, *she's really good at sucking dick*? Asshole. "Oh, really? That's nice of him. Don't believe everything you hear." I force a laugh.

She lets out a little giggle. "Don't sell yourself short, because Tick and Manny speak highly of you as well."

Well *that* part surprises me. If Tick isn't busy chasing me away from Tony, he is scowling about something. And Manny...well, let's just say if a woman isn't putting out, he doesn't have much interest.

My cheeks flush and I squirm in my seat. "They're all very sweet."

"Ha. Now, that's a first. I don't think sweet has ever been used when describing those three." She throws her head back in laughter, her black hair cascading around her shoulders.

I laugh out loud, realizing she is absolutely right. I snap my clutch shut. "You ready?"

She turns completely around to face me, her hands on her lap. "Not quite. I wanted to come in here with you to talk."

My heart plummets. Maybe she knows that I fucked her boyfriend. I dip my chin into my chest, trying to concentrate on placing a blank expression on

161

my face, before looking back up to face the firing squad.

"I think there may have been some confusion earlier when we met, and it's bothered me ever since. Especially knowing how Tony feels about you."

My eyes widen and I stare at her, waiting for her to finish. Confusion? Was I wrong in my assumption? How *does* Tony feel about me?

She smiles at me and leans in to touch my hand. "Tony is my brother. I'm afraid you may have gotten the wrong impression."

I exhale a loud breath as relief settles over me. My pounding heart settles back to its steady beat, and I place both hands to my cheeks in embarrassment. "Oh, my goodness. I've made a mess out of everything, haven't I?" For the first time, I see the resemblance between the two of them. Both have dark black hair, the same doe shaped eyes—how did I not see it before? I slap the palm of my hand to my forehead for being so stupid. "I'm such an idiot."

She laughs at my comment. "I can see how it would seem to an outsider looking in." She stops laughing and her face becomes very serious. "Tony is a very complicated man. He bears the weight of the world on his shoulders. I'm not against the two of you together, but I'll say that a relationship with you adds a complication."

I open my mouth to ask her what she means, but she holds up her hand.

"I think we've kept the boys waiting long enough." She stands and gives herself one last look in the mirror.

I push the questions aside for the moment and we walk arm and arm out of the ladies' room, back into the ballroom. There are about two hundred people, and still more are walking in. This night will be a huge success for Rheda, and I feel a rush of pride for her.

Winta gives my arm a gentle squeeze before letting go and walking off to talk with Tick and Manny.

I feel him before I see him. He bends and talks into my ear. "She told you, didn't she?" I nod, without looking at him. "I told her to let me handle it, but she insisted on having a girl talk with you. I hope you weren't blindsided."

I swallow hard and turn to face him. I open my mouth to speak, but Rheda is on the microphone, asking everyone to take their seats.

"I'm at table number one," I say to him, hoping he is seated near me.

"Fifty-two. I'll find you." He walks away.

The meal is an eight-course extravaganza of kobe beef, lobster, and caviar, each dish better than the last. I wonder about my waistline, but only for a moment before pushing those ugly thoughts out of my head and keep eating. I love good food. Rheda, as the event's hostess, has hardly taken three bites, though, because of the seemingly endless questions from staff members. After the dessert plates are removed, Rheda is back on the stage.

"Well, I hope you've all enjoyed the dishes Chef Rauch has prepared for you. Let's give him and his team a round of applause."

We all clap as he takes a bow off to the side.

"Now, is everyone ready for the auction?"

A few of the gagsters do a woot-woot as others applaud.

I preen my neck in search of the art up for auction, but again, I don't see any. Why is everyone getting so excited about bidding on art? I don't recall getting this giddy at the Christie's auctions.

"Okay, well can my first lady take the stage? Bret James, everyone!"

The woman from a few tables to my left stands and walks to the stage.

"Bret is a well-known news anchor at NBC studios. She holds a Masters in Political Science, and is a really good debater. I will start off the opening bid at five thousand."

The auction is a *people* auction? What have I agreed to? Numerous bids go into play before bidding ends at fifty thousand. Nine more women go up and are auctioned for the night. My name is the last one called.

Dread hits me, and then excitement. Tony, he will bid on me, I imagine.

I rise and walk to the podium, sweat coating the palms of my hands.

"Anaya Scott is a famous interior designer. Known all throughout the world for her fabulous creations." I blush as Rheda lays it on thick. "She is my best friend and a very intelligent woman. Let's start her opening bid at twenty thousand."

I turn to glare at Rheda. Twenty-thousand opening bid? Who the hell is going to bid over that? Rheda ignores me, as usual.

To my surprise, bids begin to flow in. Someone yells out thirty, another yell for thirty-five, and I hear sixty, but none are from the voice I want to hear. My heart drops and I fight to keep my bottom lip from quavering.

"One-hundred thousand." Tony has somehow walked up to the stage without me noticing. He gives me a wink and my stomach does a flip as my cheeks warm. The room goes quiet and most of the other bidders take a seat.

"One-twenty," Tick says from behind him.

Tony spins around and scowls at him, teeth clenched, as Tick laughs.

"One-thirty," Tony announces as oohs and ahhs are heard around the room.

"One-forty," Tick says, still chuckling. I'll jump down and kick him if he messes this up for me.

Tony shakes his head at him and mutters something that only Tick can hear, causing Tick to laugh even louder. "One-fifty," he replies through gritted teeth.

You can hear a pin drop in the room, as everyone waits to see if Tick will counter bid. Tick doesn't say anything because he is busy chuckling.

"One-fifty, going once, going twice..." Rheda says out loud.

"One-seventy," Manny calls from the back of the room.

Tony and Tick turn in his direction. Tony has a look that would make a rabid dog cry, and Tick is folded over in laughter.

"Five-hundred," Tony says out loud, his eyes slowly circling the room, fists clenched, daring any man to outbid him.

My eyes widen, along with my mouth.

"Sold!" Rheda yells into the microphone to a large round of applause in the room.

Rheda nudges me off the stage, since my feet feel as if they are glued in place. Did he really just agree to a half a million for a dance with me?

Tony and Tick give each other a bro hug before Tony walks to the side to collect his prize. He helps me down the steps of the stage and into his waiting arms.

I fight the urge to tongue the man down in front of God and country, but a knowing look passes between us. The music begins and he pulls me in closer to him, twirling me out onto the dance floor.

"I can't believe you bid that much," I chide.

"Worth every dime."

"For a dance?" I laugh.

"Yes, because you are *priceless*."

Well, that just earned the lad a panty-dropping good time—*if* he keeps playing his cards right.

I feel the bulge in his tuxedo pants, eager to greet me. I flush at the memory of his cock inside me.

"Uh, Tony?" I peek up at him through my lash extensions.

"Hmm?"

"Wanna get out of here?"

His topaz eyes darken. "Thought you'd never ask." He grabs my arm and we leave the crowded dance floor.

We make the quick trip down to the lobby and into his waiting limo. Seated on the plush leather seats, he on one end and I on the other, with just our pinkies touching in the middle, I can't deny the magnetic pull I feel for him. He reacts before I do, sliding closer to me and lifting me onto his lap, kissing me with abandon.

It feels like our two worlds are colliding to create this beautiful cosmic explosion. My skin is on fire from the electric spark between us. I might just burn up from the heat, but what a delicious burn it would be. Each stroke of his hand sends another shockwave through me, and I gasp for breath in between kisses.

"Angel, I–"

"No words Tony, no more words," I murmur in between the gentle kisses I place around his lips. I don't want to hear words from his lips, I'd rather feel them in his touch.

I feel the sudden release of my breasts as he unzips my too-tight dress and I can suddenly breathe again. I exhale from the relief of being free of the binding corset top, and the delicate silk falls to my waist. I lift off of his lap enough for him to slowly drag the dress the rest of the way down my legs, and it falls into a crumbled heap on the floor.

The fashion-conscious Anaya would've worried about a fifteen-thousand-dollar dress laying on a dirty floor, but the horny bitch Anaya doesn't give a damn, and would gladly do it all over again.

Tony's hands stroke down my back as I unbutton his shirt, the jacket removed during the elevator ride. His hands travel lower and lower and suddenly stop. I halt as well, wondering why the sudden pause. I look into his eyes and a wide smile spreads across his lips.

"No panties, Ms. Scott?" he asks playfully.

I brush my lips gently on his. "Form fitting dress, Mr. Delaney."

"Fuck me. Wish I'd known that before. We could have skipped the bidding and went straight to the limo."

I chuckle into his neck as I place tender pecks down his throat. "And Rheda would've killed both of us for the money the charity would have missed out on."

"I would've given her a blank check." He pulls me back to his chest and kisses me again before placing me on the seat, kneeling in between my legs. "I never did get to have that taste before."

Placing my legs on his shoulders, he pulls me down to the edge of the seat, and with a lascivious smile on his face, he inhales my scent. His eyes flutter like a man who is high, high off of me. I'm his drug, and he is mine. His tongue flicks out and takes one long lick of my heated center, and I'm thankful for my Brazilian wax appointment a few days ago. I let out a moan and stretch my arms out, reaching for the stars, because he is sending me into orbit.

His tongue penetrates my opening with quick thrusts, over and over again. I'm panting so hard I feel dizzy, and my skin becomes slick with sweat. "Oh my God, Tony."

I hear his zipper and the tear of a foil wrapper. I bite my bottom lip as I concentrate on all of the sensations, committing them to memory. I feel the tip of his penis spread me open, greeting him with my warmth. I exhale because it feels like home after a long day.

He kisses my lips and I smell my intoxicating scent on him. I want to devour him completely. His movements are slow and controlled, not like the wild abandon from our interlude in my office weeks ago.

It's almost foreign to me, until I realize what he is doing. He is making love to me. He is making me his. I open myself to receive him completely, and give myself to him freely. I want him to own me, possess me, and cherish me. I deserve that and, for once, I'll have it.

"Tony, I love you." There I've said it. I've laid myself bare for this man. I'm offering him, not just my body, but me. All of me.

He freezes, and his eyes widen at my admission. My heart beats steady, not that nervous anxiety one would expect. It is my truth and I would say it again. The driver bangs on the glass partition.

"Mr. Delaney. We've arrived."

Tony closes his eyes and places his sweaty forehead against my own. "We should get upstairs," he whispers before he pulls out of me. My body contracts, missing him.

We silently put on our clothes, as best we can, inside the limo. Not bothering to zip up my dress, he simply places his jacket over my shoulders. Hand in hand, the best dressed, most disheveled people take a long elevator ride to his condo, without another word between us.

Not even the words I'd hoped to hear in return: *I love you, too.*

# Chapter 14
**Without You ~ Lapalux**

Anaya

"Come on. Get up, sleepyhead." Tony playfully slaps me on the ass.

I stretch languorously in his bed. "Mmm. You're the reason why I didn't get much sleep last night." I clench my legs together at the thought of making love to him in the limo, and in his living room, the shower, the bedroom floor. Come to think of it, we never had sex on his bed. Well, that's something I'm looking to correct.

He stands by the bed, his naked goodness on full display for me. "I want to show you something." His eyes are lit like a five-year-old on Christmas day.

He looks youthful when he plays around like this. I wish to bottle up this moment and save it, like so many other memories.

I crawl to him, slowly, on all fours like a cat. I rise to my knees in front of him and pull him in for a kiss, morning breath and all.

"If we get started, we won't stop." In between each word, he kisses my lips gently. "I want to take you somewhere." He smacks my ass again, sending tingles to the very places that, just hours ago, he got well acquainted with.

I look at him with a shocked expression. "You mean, like a date?"

He blushes as he lowers his head. "Umm. Yeah. I guess so."

"Why, Tony Delaney is asking me out on a date? Be still my little girl's heart." I bat my lashes at him.

"I did do this out of order, didn't I?" He pulls me into him. "Should've asked you out first, *then* tried to get into your pants."

I brush my lips against his. "No complaints from me. But what am I going to do for clothes?"

He lifts up a bag with Saks Fifth Avenue stamped on the front. "Had someone pick up some stuff for you. Hope it fits."

I climb out of the bed and grab the bag. He thought of everything. Pants, shirt, bra, panties, and sandals. He must've had a woman do the shopping. It was definitely my style and size. "Tony, this is incredibly sweet of you. When did you have a chance to get someone to do this?"

"I sent Tallie a text and had her gather it for me. She's seen you a few times, so she knew what you liked."

He's referring to his hostess at Pulse. I place my newly purchased items on the bed and kiss him. He tries to tug me closer, but I pull away and walk toward the bathroom. I turn around, posing by the doorframe. "Coming?"

"Fuck, I hope so." He jogs over to me, picking me up, and throwing me over his shoulder.

After a wild sexcapade in the shower, we dress and leave his condo hand in hand, and I see now what a real relationship should feel like. I could do this with him forever. Downstairs, we wait for the valet to bring his car around. He kisses me passionately as passersby walk around us, some saying, "Get a room."

This public show of affection is yet another thing Iggy would never do. I've come to realize, over the past few weeks, that I've been starved for love. But Tony hasn't said he reciprocates the love I confessed to him last night. Can I enter another loveless relationship?

The valet pulls up with Tony's volcano red McLaren 650S Spider, the roof already retracted. With both doors open, it looks like angel's wings. Tony holds a door open, waiting for me to take a seat. I sit on the soft black Alcantara-covered seat, the suede-like material brushing against my skin, tickling me. He tips the valet, who yells out, "Have a great day, Mr. Delaney. Let me know if there is anything else I can do."

Tony gives him a quick salute and gets in. The valet closes the driver side door as Tony reaches across, taking my hand into his, and kissing my knuckles gently. Shivers travel up my spine from his touch and I briefly wonder if I ride him out in the open, would anyone notice? This is New York, after all. The engine purrs and Tony peels off in a quick and fluid thrust.

"Where are, we going?" I almost bounce up and down in my seat with anticipation.

He glances over at me and I want to melt. "You'll see."

Forty minutes later, we are parking in front of Totonno's Pizzeria in Coney Island.

"You're taking me for pizza?" I try not to pout as he helps me out of the car.

Swatting my ass, he retorts, "Best pizza in Brooklyn. Come on. Want you to meet my friend."

He holds the door open and I walk in.

"Tony. Good to see you. Opened early just for you and your girl." A man who looks to be in his late fifties walks around the counter to shake Tony's hand, and kiss mine.

"Clem. Thanks for opening up for me."

"It's no problem. I know what it's like to want to romance your girl. I did some crazy shit when I romanced Celia, God rest her soul." Clem looks to me and says, "Excuse my language. Ehh… Tony, introduce me."

"Anaya, this is Clemente, but call him Clem. He won't answer to anything else."

"Nice to meet you, Clem."

"Nice to meet you." He bows. I can tell that he used to be quite the catch in his day. His eyes are a dark, smoky gray, and he has naturally olive, tanned skin. "Take a seat anywhere you like and I'll get your order ready."

"Double pepperoni with sausage and anchovy?" Tony asks as he places his hand on the small of my back.

"Comin' your way." Clem throws his dishtowel over his shoulder.

The restaurant is very small, with four booths against the wall, one table that seats two in the middle aisle, and three booths against the other wall. Tony takes my hand and leads me to a booth toward the front. I slide in as he sits in across from me.

"How long have you been coming here?"

"Grew up not too far from here. So, guess you can say all of my life."

"Really? I went to Lafayette High School, down that way." I point in one direction.

"I went to Lincoln." He points his finger the other direction.

"We were practically neighbors and didn't even know it." A huge smile spreads across my face.

He reaches his hand across the table and link our fingers together. Rubbing his thumb against my skin he says, "Yeah. I wanted you to see where I came from."

Perhaps this is his way of showing me that he loves me. The lack of his words reciprocating his love to me from last night comes to mind.

"Tony, I should tell you that I'm still seeing someone. He's still away on business, but…"

"Another reason why I wanted this day with you. I want… I want to see where this can go," he replies.

"So do I. I'll have to have a talk with Iggy when he returns. I can't go on with this farce of a relationship he and I have. I want something that's real."

He squeezes my hand gently and smiles. My heart is full of emotion but my head is full of questions.

"Tony, I want to be with you. But there is so much about each other that we don't know." How do I explain Iggy's threats? "I saw someone at your club a few weeks ago."

"Who?"

"Jay. He was delivering a shipment." From the look on his face, I can tell Tick didn't mention that to him. "I take it you already know Jay's boss."

He shifts in his seat, his eyes not meeting mine.

"Ignacio is my boyfriend. Tony, I have to ask…did you know?"

He opens his mouth to speak but his cell phone rings. He presses ignore but it rings again. He looks at the screen, closes his eyes for a moment, and exhales. "Angel, I've got to take this." He reaches out to take my hands in his. "I promise to answer your question." He places the phone to his ear and stands up, walking out of the restaurant.

Clem walks over and takes a seat. I watch Tony as he speaks animatedly on the phone.

"I'm glad he found someone special. That kid has had shit for luck in his life." Clem has that old-school Brooklyn accent.

Intrigued, I turn my attention to Clem. "How so?"

"Before the death of Poppy, he used to be just a regular kid, ya know? He would come over here with his friends after school and sit at this booth for hours." He taps on the table.

"Who was Poppy?" I lean in closer.

He doesn't hear me because he's too caught up in the memories. "She was a lovely woman. Too bad she fell in love with the wrong man."

"But who was Poppy to Tony?" I speak a little louder.

"He never told you his mother's nickname?"

"Tony's mother?"

"Yeah, Vivian was a beautiful woman. Tony looks so much like her. He don't look like his father too much."

"What happened to her?"

He shakes his head as tears form in his eyes. "Suicide." He makes the sign of the cross.

A stabbing sensation goes through my heart, wounds from my childhood now reopened for Tony's grief. He knows loss the same way that I know it. "But what about his father? Was he sent to live with him?"

"No. Tony, went to live in upstate New York with his mother's sister. Old Man DeLuca didn't want no part of him."

My mouth becomes dry as I try to form coherent words. "Did you say, 'Old Man DeLuca?'"

"Yeah, you know, the Mafia boss. He was still married, but Tony's mom was his mistress. Sometimes, Ignacio would eat here, too. Never did like that kid. Mean son of a bitch."

My head feels like a pressure cooker that is ready to explode. I lift my hands and place my finger tips to my temples and rub. "Tony and Iggy are brothers?" I say, more to myself than anyone else.

The bell on the door chimes and I look up to see Tony walking in. Our gazes lock for what seems like an eternity. I feel like my movements are in slow motion as my hands lower to the table and my eyes narrow at him. His forehead crinkles in confusion from my glare. My heart that, just a few minutes ago pounded with love for him, now pounds with fury.

"Oh, Tony, I was just telling your girlfriend here about the old times." Clem stands. "I'll get that pizza out for you."

Tony bends to kiss me but I turn my head. Wordlessly, he takes a seat in front of me. "Sorry about that. It was Tick. He was giving me an update on some news I was waiting for."

"Oh?" My voice is slightly higher in pitch as I try to control my warring emotions. "Like the news of Ignacio being your brother?" My lips purse as I stare at him, rage pushing me to finish. "Or perhaps the news that you fucking knew I was dating Iggy all along? Or, let's try something else; I'm leaving and I never want to see you again." I grab my purse and stand to leave. My bottom lip trembles as I fight back the tears that want to come.

Tony grabs my wrist but I yank it out of his grasp. "Angel, wait. I can explain."

I'm already throwing the door open. "The time for you to explain would have been before I sucked your dick, Tony!" I step outside and into what feels like a wall of heat. Beads of sweat form on my forehead and I wipe at them with the back of my shaky hand.

He jogs after me down the street. "Angel, baby, please stop."

*Ignore him and keep walking, Anaya. Fuck him!*
But then he says something that causes the ground to be snatched from under me.

"I'm going to kill Ignacio."

# Chapter 15
**Tennessee Whiskey ~ Chris Stapleton**

Tony

She stops walking and slowly turns around, staring at me with her large, brown eyes. Did time suddenly freeze?

"Wh-what?" *Can't go back now.*

"I said, I'm going to kill Ignacio." I repeat the words slowly as I walk toward her.

She takes a step back. "Y-you can't. Why?"

Minutes ago, she looked at me with love and now it's been replaced by shock and horror. I would rather be stabbed than to have that look on her face directed at me.

"I can and I will." She flinches when I hold my hand out to her. Instantly I place my hand back at my side. These are the same hands that held her close to me as we slept last night and now she is scared for me to touch her. I feel gutted like I've never felt before. I clear my throat. "Let me explain."

She stares, not at me, but through me.

"Angel, I'd never hurt you. I think you know that."

She closes her eyes for a moment and then opens them, walks past me and back to the restaurant. I follow behind her like a man walking his final steps to the electric chair.

We sit at the booth, with her glaring, while I'm wishing Clem wasn't such a damn gossip.

"Well?" She crosses her arms in front of her as I debate how to tear open old wounds.

"My mother grew up in Brighton Beach, a few blocks from here. She met my father, Old Man DeLuca, when she was seventeen. She had me when she was eighteen." I grab a paper napkin from the dispenser and throw my concentration into tearing it into tiny shreds…like my fractured life.

"Winta is his daughter, too?"

My gaze flies up to meet hers. "No. Mom found out he was married and broke things off with him

189

before I was born. She dated this guy who got drafted into the NBA, and had Winta. But that relationship didn't last either because he traveled a lot. It really didn't take much for my father to figure out that I was his. He insisted on being a part of my life. Even going as far as telling his wife about me, and making sure Ignacio and I grew up as brothers."

Her eyes lower. "Oh."

I need her to understand everything so I push forward with the story. "You see, Winta and I have always been close. We were what people called Irish Twins. When my father would pick me up on weekends, she would tag along too."

"I see."

I clear my throat. "Ignacio and I are the same age. He's always had a thing for Winta. One day I caught the way he looked at her and I beat the shit out of him."

"I know Ignacio. He wouldn't have taken that lightly."

"And he didn't. He, uh…he took it out on Winta instead." I drop the remains of the shredded napkin on the table and press my hands to my face. If it wasn't for me, Winta wouldn't have been hurt.

"Tony? What did he do to Winta?"

"I had football practice after school. He waited for her. Told her that I told him to walk her home." I swallow down the memories and force myself to finish the story. "She didn't think anything of it because he had walked her home before. But this time, Ignacio had other things on his mind."

Her hands fly to her mouth. "Oh my God. He raped her, didn't he?" she sobs.

Unable to speak, I just nod.

"But, I don't understand. Why did your mother kill herself?"

"My father threatened my mother; he'd kill her if she pressed charges against Ignacio. Winta's father was furious and took Winta away from us."

"And that's when…"

191

"Yeah." I wipe a tear from my eye. "It's funny how you can have a normal day at school. You know, bullshitting with your friends and trying to get a girl's number. Shit like that, that makes the day seem so normal. Shot some hoops with the boys and hung out here at this very booth. When she…she was upstairs, dying."

I take the fork and scrape it across the wooden table. Marking it the way I've been marked for years now. "Had I not hung out, I might have been there in time." I look up to see Anaya staring at me with tears in her eyes.

"Do you know how many times I asked myself that damn question? 'What if I had just come home?' There isn't a day that goes by I don't wake up with that question on my mind." That question, along with the sight of her body.

"I arrived home, my usual time, around seven. My curfew was seven-thirty." This part is the only part that isn't easy to tell. The moment I opened that door, my life would forever be changed. My hands clench into fists on top of the table.

"The moment I opened that door, I knew something wasn't right." I look up to see Anaya waiting patiently for me to rip open those old wounds. I grind my teeth together, unsure if I can finish.

I inhale and close my eyes, instantly bringing myself back to that evening. "The apartment was dark and quiet." I remember sniffing the air for the smell of dinner, but all I smelled was the stale scent of the fried bacon and eggs she had prepared for me that morning before school.

My throat feels like it has moth balls in it. I open my eyes and reach for the glass of water, taking a sip. The water hitting my empty stomach makes me instantly nauseous, and I set the glass down and push it away. "I called out 'Mom' a few times, but nothing."

A bead of sweat falls down the side of my face. I wipe it away with a wayward flick of the hand. "Something told me then."

I look at her again, tears in her eyes. "I just knew it." My voice is a whisper. The memory of me slowly walking down the long hallway of our apartment, occasionally stopping, because I was too much of a chicken shit to face what was about to become my new reality. Her door was slightly ajar and I could see her feet on her bed. I must've stood at that fucking door an hour before I pushed it all the way open to see her body laying peacefully on top of the covers.

I used to love horror movies when I was a teenager, and death always looked so fucking brutal. Never did I think seeing my mother lying dead in her bed would look almost serene. Like she was having a good dream before she would wake up and ask me, "Tony, how was your day?" and give me that sloppy kiss on the cheek I'd always wipe away. Fuck. I'd kill to have my mother kiss me on the cheek one last time.

"She looked like she was sleeping. But I knew she wasn't." I'd bent to pick up the empty bottle of Percocet that her doctor prescribed for her from a car accident-related back injury the year before.

"You ever know someone and just knew they wouldn't be with you forever?" I'd grabbed that damn letter that was lying next to her. "Can you believe I actually got a fucking 'Dear Tony' letter from my mother? It wasn't an apology. It was just saying goodbye, and that she loved me." I begin reciting the words that are forever etched in my memory.

My Dear Sweet Tony,

I can't go on like this anymore. Life has no more meaning for me. I tried, you know how I struggled every day. Because of me, your sister's innocence is lost. Because of me, we are no longer a family. I pray the two of you can forgive me one day.

Love you always, from eternity and back,

Mom

"Oh my God." She holds a trembling hand to her lips. It's the same hand I kissed in the car on the way here and I wonder, for a moment, if she will ever let me taste her sweet lips again.

"I swore, on that day, that I'd kill Ignacio."

I stare at her and watch her take in everything I said. I've bared my soul for her.

"Now, I have a question for you."

"What?" Her eyes are questioning.

"Will you help me?"

# Chapter 16
**Strange Love ~ Halsey**

Anaya

I remember I was once stuck in Macy's elevator on 34th Street in Manhattan a few years ago. That was forty minutes of pure horror, alone with just my crazy imagination. It felt like the walls were closing in around me, sucking the air out of the small space. I prayed that the firemen would get to me before I passed out. I steadied myself, leaning against those aluminum walls, thankful for the coolness against my hot skin. When the fireman finally got me out, he said I was one lucky young woman, even as the feeling of death was still surrounding me. And here I am, sitting in a pizzeria in Brooklyn, that same feeling from that day rushing back to me.

"What did you just say?" I blink rapidly, waiting for him to utter any words other than what I refuse to believe he just said.

"You heard me, Angel. I'm not asking you to pull a trigger. I'm asking you if you'll keep quiet."

"Is that the reason you slept with me? To make me your accomplice?" My skin feels flushed in the small restaurant. I reach for a napkin from the dispenser and dab it in the glass of water before pressing it against my skin.

"No. It's not that way at all." His voice is guarded, and he's studying my every movement. I debate flipping him the bird. Let him commit *that* to memory.

"Really? It sure looks that way from where I'm sitting." I toss the napkin carelessly on the table, my jaw firmly set.

He closes his eyes for a moment. "I tried to walk away from you."

*Does he want a fucking medal?* "Why did you request me to redesign Pulse, Tony?"

He looks away.

"I guess I got my answer." I gather up my things so I can haul ass out of here and away from this shit. The headache of all headaches is threatening to appear.

He reaches out his hand but my glare makes him place it back on the table. "Wait. No. I did ask you to work at Pulse to get at Ignacio. At first."

"So, you intended to use me? What were you going to do? Tell Ignacio that I fucked you? You thought that would break him? Puh-leez. Ignacio and I haven't had sex in—I don't know how long. It wouldn't have crushed him, but it would be a death sentence for me."

His face falls the way my heart did at his admission.

"You didn't care, did you? You knew he'd kill me for sleeping with you, and you didn't care."

"That's not true."

"Oh my fucking God. How could I fall for two animals like you? What am I, a masochist?"

"Angel, it wasn't like that. I didn't factor in falling for you."

"What, Tony? Are you telling me you love me? Last I checked, we've just been fucking. It was good sex, I'll give you that. But not once did we have an in-depth conversation. What are my favorite foods? Songs? Colors? You don't know me, and you just proved I damn sure don't know you." I stand, my bag in hand.

"Wait. You told me you loved me last night."

"Yeah, that was before I realized you were using me." I can't breathe, the air in this room feels like it's being sucked out.

"I want that chance to get to know you. I want to…"

"Want to what, Tony?" I gasp, clutching my chest.

"Just give me a chance."

"Whatever, Tony." I storm toward the door. "I won't say anything to Iggy. But you stay the hell away from me or I swear I'll sing like a goddamn canary."

The warm air hits me, or is that my temper rising? Finally, I can inhale and breathe again. I concentrate on taking calming breaths I learned in the one yoga class I attended. Having grown up not too far from here, I walk in the direction of the boardwalk. Since this is a summer weekday, there are mostly teenagers out and about on the streets. I walk the few blocks past the train station and Nathan's hot dogs, and up the ramp of the boardwalk. I take a seat and look out at the ocean.

I feel him standing behind me. I just don't have the energy anymore.

"I thought I told you to stay away from me."

"Angel, can I sit?" His voice is pleading.

"If I told you no, would you go away?" My voice is one of defeat.

He sits down next to me. "It really wasn't the way it sounded. I wanted you to work at the club to keep closer tabs on Ignacio. I wasn't going to seduce you to hurt him."

"And why should I believe you?" Tears fall freely down my cheeks and I don't bother to wipe them away. Let him see what he has done to me.

"I had the opportunity to tell him weeks ago and I didn't. I tried pushing you away and you know that."

"What do you want from me?" My vision blurred from the tears, I turn to look at him.

"I want a chance to prove I'm a good man. I want us to discover each other."

"Discover each other? Ha. Whatever you're selling, I'm not buying." I turn back to look at the ocean.

"I know you're hurt. I'll give you the time you need. Just don't give up on me yet. Please."

"I don't know. I've been hurt before, by your brother. I don't think I can put myself out there again, not for you. Especially knowing everything."

"I won't push it any further." He stands. "Come on. I'll take you home."

I shift in my seat. "I can find my own way back."

He stares at me a moment longer before walking away.

# Chapter 17
**Studio ~ Schoolboy Q**

Tony

Sitting in my office, I stare out at the empty dance floor, sipping on my medicine of choice, scotch. My third glass this hour, and I'm still waiting for the amber liquid to erase my memories. Maybe I'm not drinking fast enough. I lift the glass to my lips to get another taste and see emptiness where liquid should be.

The memory of my fight with Anaya hits me and my muscles tense as I grasp the glass tighter. Fuck! How did I fuck everything up? Tick warned me to stay the hell away from her. He cautioned me to keep my head in the game. But there was something about her. Her large warm, brown eyes reminded me of a time in my life when I was happy. When I had a mother who was there for me. A sister who wasn't brutalized because of me. Looking at her, I was reminded of all that I'd lost and all that I want in my life again.

I've been consumed with a need for revenge that it took over the missing components of my life. Briefly knowing Anaya gave it all back to me. Now I've lost it, yet again. I sometimes wonder, if I split my chest open, would it reveal a heart or a black hole where one should be.

My office door swings open and Tick and Manny stroll in as if they own the fucking joint. Assholes.

Manny takes his usual seat, making himself at home, kicking his feet up on my desk. He lights his cigarette and blows out a smoke ring. "What's up?"

I look over at Tick, who is leaning against the wall near the wet bar. Figures, the cocksucker would position himself by the booze.

I rise, knowing I'll need another drink for this conversation, and walk over to pour myself a glassful of scotch. Why bother to measure at this point? "We're going to have to speed things up a bit. Anaya knows everything."

I met Tick after my mother died and I moved in with her sister Carol, in upstate New York. We lived a few houses down from each other. So basically, I guess you can say we know each other pretty well. He is like a brother to me, more so than Ignacio has ever been. I gauge his expression, and I know what is on his mind, but he won't say it. *I told you so.* Those four words hover over our heads to be tucked away for another time, when we are sitting back with a beer and we can laugh about it.

"Fuck."

Leave it to Manny to break up the dramatic effect of a bombshell moment.

"I spoke with Ignacio this morning. He's due back in New York any day now."

"What line did you feed him to get him back?" Tick asks.

"Told him that I might have a handle on whose been hitting his warehouses." Of course, it's my men hitting his storage facilities, but since I'd been with Anaya, I laid off on the attacks over the past few weeks. My head was no longer in the game, because everything about her consumed me.

"We should just send someone out to Miami and kill him." Manny sits upright in the chair.

"No. I have better plans for him."

"Should be no problem moving things up." Tick takes the empty chair and sits, kicking his feet up on my desk.

*What's with these two always putting their feet on my desk?*

"What about Anaya? She going to talk?" Manny, who has just finished one smoke, searches for another.

"She said she won't."

"You trust that?" He now searches for his lighter.

"With my fucking life," I growl.

"Did you tell her about that other thing?" Tick asks warily.

"No. I already ripped the rug out from under her. Didn't want to do more damage."

"You serious about her?" Tick sits up straight.

"Yeah."

"Then let me clue you in on something. Full fucking disclosure. Tell her everything or lose her." Tick dishes out advice like a short order cook.

"I can't do that."

"Horse shit. You don't want to do it because you're a fucking pussy." He points his index finger in my direction.

For the first time in my life, I want to punch Tick. I want to slam my fist down his fucking throat.

"I hate it when mommy and daddy fight," Manny jokes around.

The tension between Tick and I dissolves as we laugh at Manny.

"Should I put eyes on Anaya?"

"No. She should be safe. Ignacio has no reason to harm her."

"Alright."

Manny and Tick both stand to leave but Tick gives me a parting message. "You really need to tell her sooner rather than later."

Damned if I didn't know he was right.

# Chapter 18
**Gimme Shelter ~ Rolling Stones**

Anaya

I sit in Chelsea's office, waiting for her to get off the phone. Her back is to me as she schmoozes, in her sugary sweet voice, a client. I wonder if they realize she's just being fake. Everything about her is fake—from her eyelashes to her butt implants she is rumored to have gotten.

She finally hangs up, after I've been sitting and sweating it out for twenty minutes. I did wonder briefly if she was really on the phone, or perhaps just wanting to show that she is the boss and I'm just a squirrel trying to get a nut in this world. She'll toss me the discarded shells if she chooses to.

Spinning around, she busies herself with some paperwork on her desk, not bothering to acknowledge me for minutes longer.

I clear my throat in hopes of her looking up, but she seems unfazed. Bitch is probably actually timing how long she should keep me waiting.

"Okay, tell me Anaya. What do you need?" The queen speaks from high up on her throne to her mere subject, not bothering to look at me as she picks up another sheet of paper to read.

I had my entire speech planned out this morning. I thought long and hard about it last night, after I got home from my fucked-up day with Tony. But now, sitting here, the words seem to have left my mind. Fuck!

She peeks up at me, glaring. "Well?"

"Uh," is all I manage to say, hoping it will buy me some time. Okay, option one. I keep working on the Pulse project. I stay out of Tony's way and he mine. I get it done in record time and go my merry way. Option two, I tell Chelsea I can no longer work at Pulse. I give her a bullshit excuse that escapes me at the moment and basically throw away my career and everything that I worked so hard to achieve.

Last night, I chose option two. It made sense to me in my fit of anger. But now, I'm not so sure any more. How about option three? I run away from it all, never to be heard from again.

Damn it. I know what I have to do.

"I, uh, thought I'd give you an update on Pulse."

Chelsea's face brightens, or is that her chemical peel that makes her look that way? She places the paperwork back on her desk, smiling at me. "Yes, I heard from Tony today, and he said it is going well."

She heard from Tony? I wonder if she is in on his scheme to use me.

"Well, I'm glad that he is pleased." I try to sound even-toned but I'm pretty sure my face twitched a little.

"He is. And if he's pleased, then I'm pleased. If I'm pleased, then you should be pleased because you get to keep your job."

She just had to stick that part in there, didn't she? I open my mouth to say some bullshit nicety but she buzzes her secretary, informing her that I'm leaving now.

Taking my dismissal cue, I stand to leave. Okay Anaya, that didn't go according to plan. I can do this, can't I? I can work on Pulse and not cross paths with him. I can…right?

The hell I can. I need a drink and I know just the person who can help me.

An hour later, I'm pulling up to the curb in a cab, with the ingredients for martinis and Jack and Coke. I plan on drinking myself into a decision, and Rheda's going to help me. She just doesn't know it.

I pay the cab fare and carry my burdens toward her brownstone in a trendy section of Harlem's Sugar Hill.

"Anaya?"

I stop, turning around to see Manny getting out of his car, parked across the street.

What is he doing here? Is Tony having him follow me?

"Manny?" I look around to see if Tony is going to step out from behind a tree or something.

"Yeah, listen, why don't you come with me instead? Tony has some design questions." He walks around the car, holding the passenger door open for me. Design questions? I've only ever dealt with Tick regarding the designs, so why would he send Manny? Unless...

Suspicions heightened, my throat feels as if it's closing up. I drop the bags as glass breaks and liquid streams down the cracks of the sidewalk. I run—in my stilettos. Not the brightest idea I've had, since I'm not really a runner, and most certainly not in stilettos.

He runs behind me and gains on me fast. I screech as various passersby look at us in wonderment. Damn it! I knew I should've been working out more rather than eating and drinking most weekends. And just like in a goddamn horror movie, my shoe gets caught in a crack in the sidewalk and gravity takes its course.

Now I'm thankful that I couldn't run that fast and he was able to catch up with me, since he breaks my fall, swooping me into his arms just before I faceplant.

As I fumble to catch my breath, I lean my head on his shoulder, before remembering why I ran in the first place.

"Please, don't kill me," I plead for my life. For heaven's sake, I'm only twenty-six years old. I have so much to live for and many more cocktails to consume.

"I'm not here to kill you." He laughs at my absurdity.

I push away from him and scowl. "Then what the hell is this all about? Why are you following me?"

He looks down at the ground. "It's not what you think."

"What do you want?"

He holds his hands up. "Seriously, I don't mean you any harm."

He keeps looking behind him in the direction we just came from.

"Well, I'm on my way to see Rheda. And you owe me money for the booze." I try to step around him.

He blocks my path.

"Manny, wh—" I never get a chance to finish what I was about to say, which would have been an expletive-laden rant. My eyes zero in on what I now realize he was blocking me from.

Rheda comes out of her brownstone in a slinky black dress that looks like or as if it's been sewn on, and she has a very interesting accessory.

Iggy.

# Chapter 19

**I Want Your Love ~ Toadies**

**Anaya**

My wide eyes feel like they're going to pop out of my head as I stare at my best friend and my boyfriend together. His arm is around her naturally thin waist. Her curls bounce as she throws her head back in laughter at something he has said. He never told me any jokes; at least none that were funny. She seems to fit so perfectly in his arms that I have to search my memory for a time when I was in her place. They walk down the street together, whispering to each other. I wonder what they are saying. Perhaps, "Oh that idiot, Anaya, has yet to figure us out." Ha. The laughs on them, I say to myself. They step over the broken bottles that I dropped only moments ago.

Manny, who is standing next to me, is forgotten, and the only people who exist are the two of them. In my mind, I fly off in a blind rage, slapping her and punching him. I would take my shoe and gouge his eyes out with the heel. And with my blood-soaked heel, I would hit her upside her head repeatedly until I saw brain matter.

I visualize this in my mind and eventually throw my head back in a laugh. One that comes up from my toes, into my stomach, and out of my mouth until it sounds like a roar. Manny stares at me in disbelief.

"Come with me. I'll take you to Tony." He reaches out to touch me but I slap his hand away.

He is spoiling my moment, after all. Am I not entitled to stand here like a madwoman?

Eventually, my laughter dies down and disappears into the breeze that passes over us. Two tears fall down my cheeks; one for a loss of a friend and the other for a relationship that had been dead for years. I catch those tears with my thumb and stare at them, committing them to memory. This moment, along with the two tears shed, deserves to be remembered, doesn't it?

"I'll call Tony." Manny reaches for his cell and I have to fight the urge not to smack it out of his hand.

"You'll do no such thing. You'll take me home."

"But—"

I turn to glare at him and the look I give has this muscular man shrinking backward. "I said, you'll take me home."

Wordlessly, he nods and we walk in silence back to his car. We pass by Rheda's brownstone and I give it one last glance.

Manny holds the passenger door open for me and I look into his eyes.

"He knew, didn't he?"

He doesn't answer me, but his silence speaks volumes.

Manny drives me home, not bothering to annoy me with things like conversation. He doesn't even turn on the radio. His phone buzzes a few times and his car's Bluetooth shows Tick, and eventually Tony, calling him. I'll be forever in his debt for ignoring the calls.

He insisted on walking me upstairs, but I won the argument. I suspect Manny has never dealt with a woman on the verge of losing her fucking mind. So he treats me with kid gloves, as if I would break.

Again, I want to laugh. I'm not fragile. Never have been. If you've been through the shit I have, you would be tougher than whip leather. And that's what I am, tough.

I barely acknowledge Fred; no time for our usual banter back and forth. A look of hurt shows on his face but I'm too numb to care.

I get off the elevator and walk into my penthouse, my last trip here. I look around the house and, again, commit everything to memory. I won't be back. I'll miss my home but not my life.

Two hours and a good cry later, I'm packed, my bags are in the vestibule waiting for Fred to pick up. I've called for a town car to take me to the airport. I debated if I should leave Iggy a "Dear John" letter but realize he isn't worth the ink.

I'm making the last of my travel arrangements, flight, hotel, and things of that nature, in my office, and I miss the sound of the front door opening. I'm so caught up in my own head that I don't hear him call out my name or his footsteps coming toward my office.

I look up from my laptop and gasp, startled to see Iggy standing in front of me.

"What the fuck is going on? Why is your suitcase packed?"

I slam my laptop shut. *The son of a bitch has the nerve to question me?* Fuck him. I unplug my laptop and place it in my briefcase.

"Today is not the day to test me, Anaya."

*Oh, now that's rich.* "Today's not the day to test *me*, Iggy," I say through gritted teeth.

I try to push past him so I can get the hell out of here. He grabs my arm and I turn around, slapping him with everything I have. The pain shoots through my wrist and my hand tingles. A large red splotch of a handprint appears on his cheek. His eyes narrow as he lunges for me.

His hand grips my neck as he pushes me against the wall. His face is so close to mine I can smell her on him. I gag, partially because he is closing off my air supply and partially because he disgusts me. Instinctively, I grab his wrists and try to remove his hands from my neck. But he is too strong and my efforts are for naught.

"It's time you learn some fucking manners around here." He knocks my head against the wall with each word.

I whimper out in pain. My God. This is it. He's going to kill me. That's when the fighter in me comes out. I claw at his face, eventually hitting him in the eye, and he releases me. I make a run for it. My mind is confused, and I'm not sure I'll even make it to the elevator. I stumble and wish I took off these damn stilettos. I skid down the hallway, grasping the wall to steady myself.

*Anaya, you can do this. You can make it to the elevator.* He grabs my hair from behind and yanks me backward. My ass hits the floor and a sharp pain shoots up my spine. Tears fall down my cheeks as my heart thunders in my chest.

*You're going to die. He's going to cover it up. No one will miss you. You have no family to mourn your loss.* God, how pathetic that I don't have a soul who would miss me.

He drags me down the hall by my hair as my hands reach up and grasp his own. I wonder, for a moment, if this is how it feels to be scalped alive? The nerve endings in my roots are burning and I cry out in pain.

"You fucking bitch. Treated you too fucking good. That's the problem." He eventually lets my hair go when we enter the bedroom.

I fall backward, my head hitting the floor with a thud.

"Why won't you let me go?" My voice is hoarse, and I wince in pain.

"I own you. If you leave, it's in a body bag." His voice is eerily calm. I would've thought when one threatens someone, it would be in a yell or a shout. But this is so much scarier. These are not just words he is speaking; it's a promise. A shudder goes through my body as I try to crawl to the wall. I firmly place my back against it and keep my eyes on him.

*Think, Anaya. You have to get out of here. Think!*

The gun! He keeps a gun in his nightstand drawer.

Should I make a run for it? I weigh my options and figure that my odds are best to keep edging toward the door.

"Iggy, please." A cry escapes my lips. "Let me go." My voice quavers.

He paces the floor in front of me like a feral beast. Large welts have formed across his face from where I scratched and clawed at him. That, at least, gives me some satisfaction. Let it be known that I didn't go down without a fight.

Slowly, ever so slowly, I edge my body toward the door. I look down at my feet and see that the straps from my shoes have cut into my skin and I'm bleeding.

Perhaps I can distract him enough so I can remove my shoes. I weigh all my options and every decision leads back to the same conclusion. *You die. Game over.*

I move my hands to the straps of my heels and undo the fastenings on one, slide the shoe off, and then go to work on the other. Iggy doesn't notice as he is still raging from our fight.

"Treated you too good. That's the problem. Didn't set you straight." He snarls.

*Set me straight?* I stand up slowly, my back still against the wall. My fear of him, and of death, is pushed out of my mind as a blind rage hits me. "You bedded half of New York, including my best friend, and you're talking about setting *me* straight? Let me set *you* straight. I won't put up with this! *I've. Had. Enough!*" My anger boils over and I see red. Years, I've put up with his infidelity. Years, I've put up with his cruelty. Years, I've put up with *everything*. I'd rather die than keep up this farce.

It's as if I flipped a switch and all the lights came on after being in the dark for so long. We stare at each other, perhaps seeing each other for the first time. Only our heavy breaths can be heard in the silent room.

For a brief moment, I thought I saw something in his eyes. Humanity, maybe?

But just like that, it's gone, replaced by something I've never seen before. Hatred? Disgust? And it's directed toward me.

It's *directed* toward me. As I try to adjust to my new reality, he reaches for his pants button and undoes it. Fear grips me and I can't feel my legs, even though I know I'm still standing.

"You want to fuck? Is that it?" His pants drop to the floor and his dick is erect.

For years, that used to be a game for us. We would argue and he would fuck me into submission. But this is not the same. I did that willingly. This is entirely different.

"Iggy. I-I don't want to." My voice sounds weak, too weak.

"*Iggy. I don't want to.*" He mimics my words as he stalks toward me.

I edge my way closer to the door. He lunges and I run for it, but he catches me by the waist, hoisting me up and throwing me onto the bed. I bounce hard and my head snaps back, causing a sharp pain in my neck.

The gun. I throw my body toward the drawer, grabbing the pewter handle. The drawer opens with ease as if this were a normal day. But it's not, is it? He notices instantly and tries to grab the gun, but I reach it first.

I hold the .38 caliber in my trembling hands. Iggy commissioned a special ivory handle with his name engraved in gold. The weight of it seems too much to hold as I take aim at him.

"You fucking bitch. You'll shoot me?"

I'm not sure what thoughts went through my head when I grabbed for the gun. Shooting him wasn't one of them. I just wanted him to leave me alone. But I pause a moment too long and that's all it takes. A cold-blooded killer like Iggy can sense another killer, and he knows he's the only one that lives in this house.

That same look of disgust passes across his face as he takes a step closer to me and the gun.

"Shoot." His voice is low and calm. No fear at all.

"I will." My hands tremble harder, betraying me.

Another step closer toward me, closing the gap. The barrel is pointed at his stomach. Our gazes lock and I try to search for the Iggy that I used to know. I did know him, didn't I? But he isn't there. He is gone, along with his patience.

He grabs the gun by its barrel and yanks it out of my hand. "Forgot to take the safety off." Iggy holds the gun up in the air as if to taunt me, like a kid would. But he doesn't forget. He flips the safety off and aims it at me.

I crawl to the other side of the bed and curl myself into the leather padded headboard.

"Iggy. Please," I beg. "What are you doing?" I plead, my voice barely above a whisper.

He climbs on the bed and walks over to me on his knees, gun still aimed at me. His free hand reaches out and grabs my foot, pulling hard. My head hits the nightstand as my body is dragged to the middle of the bed. He bends down to kiss me but I bite his lip.

"Fucking bitch!" he yells as blood trickles down his chin.

The coppery taste of his blood makes me queasy and I spit it out. His nostrils flare and his eyes narrow to tiny slits. He growls out something indecipherable. Panic goes through me as a thought of, *"This is it,"* goes through my mind.

He raises the gun high in the air before bringing it down on my head, over and over. Everything fades to black.

# Chapter 20

## Paint it Black ~The Rolling Stones

### Anaya

Lying in the bed listening to Ignacio snore lightly, I stare blankly out our bedroom window, watching the sunrise. The sun comes up, as if the day is a normal day. People will get up and get ready for work. They will sip their coffee as the morning news talks about the bad things that happened to good people the night before. A wife and husband will hug their children and be thankful that their doors were locked, shutting out the evil.

But what happens when the evil sleeps in the bed next to you? I shut my eyes at the normalcy of it all. Will I ever be able to look at a sunrise the same again?

I lift my hand and touch the large bump on top of my forehead where the butt of his gun hit me repeatedly. The skin is scabbed over, and I wince when I touch it. Sticking out my tongue, I feel for the cut on my bottom lip. More dried blood.

I try to shift my position in the bed but my body screams at me so I stop moving, waiting for the pain to subside. It doesn't. The pain is deeper than aches and pains from cuts and bruises. My soul aches as well, and I feel broken.

Losing my mother from a drug overdose didn't break me. Finding my father dead in our bathroom with a goddamned needle in his arm didn't break me. But Iggy...Iggy broke me. I'm undone and I can't ever be put back together again.

Somewhere in the room, Iggy's cell phone rings. His favorite ringtone of "Highway to Hell" blares. I feel him stir in his sleep and eventually the bed dips as he sits up. My back is still facing him and I close my eyes tighter, hoping not to bring his attention back to me.

"Yeah?" His voice is groggy and he lets out a loud yawn. All of this would have been part of normal routine as well, but normal has vacated this house and left a "For Rent" sign in its place.

"Gotta shower first. Be there in an hour." I feel the phone bounce on the bed behind me.

He yawns again and walks to the bathroom, closing the door behind him. Only when I hear the shower jets, do I open my eyes. I stare at the door, the nothingness of it all. Because that's what it is, nothing. I feel nothing, yet I know I should. I want to cry, not from the pain but for what I have lost.

The shower jets stop as abruptly as they started only minutes ago. I close my eyes tight and pray to go unnoticed until he leaves. The bathroom door slams open, but I refuse to flinch or give him another reaction. He's taken enough from me already. I won't give him this, too.

Drawers open and close with force, and eventually there's a rustling of clothes being put on.

"Shower or something. You look like fucking shit." He slams the bedroom door behind him.

Slowly, I move the sheets covering most of my wounds. The sheets that were once white now have brownish stains, tainted from last night. I sit up in the bed and bite back the shocking pain from sitting on my ass. Eventually the pain dulls a bit and I stare at the bite marks on my breasts. A sob escapes my lips. I move my legs and position myself to stand. I want to see what he has done, as it will forever be committed to memory.

I walk—no, limp—my way to my floor length mirror in my closet. I close my eyes and reach for the light switch. Yet another action in a day that should've been otherwise normal. The switch makes a loud click, startling me as memories of Iggy flipping the safety switch on the gun come to mind. My eyes spring open at the sound and I look into the mirror at the stranger staring back.

My hair is matted from sweat and blood, and I begin to analyze my wounds. My lip is split and the gaping wound on my forehead are from the repeated hits from the gun barrel, I gather. The bite marks on my breasts and thighs must have been when I was knocked out as well.

But Iggy, ever the courteous one splashed water on my face to wake me up for the other things he had in store for me.

*"Wake up, bitch. Don't want you to sleep through this."* I cringe as I remember his words and his

hot breath on my ear, bent behind me, as I lay face down on the bed.

I stare at the dried blood and semen down my thighs, the memory of my screams, dulled by the gag he had placed in my mouth.

My wrists are raw from the rope he tied my hands with last night. Yet another surprise he had for me.

Throughout the years, Iggy would ask me for anal sex but I always refused. He would get upset but eventually stopped pushing for it. That was, until last night when he slammed his dick inside of my ass like a jackhammer. Only my muffled sobs and his grunts sounded in the room.

My reality comes crashing down around me. How did I not see this coming? What is wrong with me? Why did I provoke him? I made him angry, and this is the result.

I grab the mirror and toss it to the carpeted floor. It doesn't have the desired effect of shattering, reminiscent of my devastated life. No, the plush carpeting absorbs the fall, and I don't even get a loud thump.

My mind is now on a singular focus. That mirror must break; it will be broken. I snatch one of my heels from the shelf and kneel down on the floor. I bang and bang, hit and hit, until tiny cracks form on the mirror. Nothing. I feel nothing but I want to feel again. I hit the cracks until they become bigger and bigger, eventually skewing my reflection.

I fall backward and land on my butt; pain shoots through me and I yell. Yelling feels good. It feels cleansing. I yell some more, until my voice begins to crack and my throat becomes dry. Is there anyone to hear my screams? Anyone to take away the pain? I feel as if I've been swallowed up by a spiraling black hole, heading deeper into the depths of...nowhere.

I'm tired, oh God, I'm so tired. Why didn't he kill me? I'm already dead on the inside. I feel like rotten meat that should've been discarded weeks ago. I just want the pain to end, but it won't, will it? Eventually, my wounds will heal, and people will look at me and think my life is perfect. But what about my scars? The scars that I carry in my heart? How do I heal those?

My thoughts drift back to last night and finally settle on the one thing that can save me. I stand on firm legs and walk into the bedroom. My eyes wander around the room before settling on the crumpled, bloody sheets. How can it be, that a simple change of laundry can put everything back to rights? I walk toward Ignacio's nightstand and find the object I am looking for. Of course, he would leave it out in the open. He knows he has broken me. Why fear Anaya would do anything with it now, when she didn't have the courage to use it when it counted. I'm not a cold-blooded murderer like him because, in spite of everything, I thought there might still be something worth saving in him.

I reach for the gun calmly. Whereas yesterday it felt heavy in my hands, today it feels light, as if it always belonged there. I lift the cold metal and point. I feel as if I'm in a daze, as if I took mushrooms or something, and all the colors begin to swirl together.

This time I remember to turn the safety off. I cock the hammer and pull the trigger.

# Chapter 21

## Morphine ~ Michael Jackson

## Tony

Manny, Tick, and I are in my office at Pulse, having a meeting. When I say meeting, I mean me screaming at the top of my lungs, basically foaming at the mouth.

"One more time. Why didn't you put a bullet in his fucking head?" My fists slam on the desk, rattling various items, and an uncapped water bottle topples over and spills all over my papers. *Great, just fucking great.*

"You wanted me to kill him in front of her? Don't think she would have appreciated that shit." Manny stands his ground as he searches his pocket, eventually pulling out a pack of cigarettes.

I growl at him. I might end up killing this fucking kid before those cancer sticks do the job.

"Listen, losing your shit right now isn't helping anything. Manny was right. He couldn't kill Ignacio when she was there. You would've done the same thing in his place." Ticks stands in front of Manny and faces me. "Think about it."

I rub my hands through my hair. Fuck. He's right. *Hate it when he's right.* "She won't answer her phone." My voice is a low rumble. "Why won't she answer her phone?"

"It might be because you're the one who is calling. You said she didn't take that news too well." Tick reminds me of my discussion with Anaya at the pizzeria a few days ago.

A thought hits me, and I grab my cell and dial a number quickly. "Yeah, is Anaya in today?"

Chelsea's voice sounds like a wannabe Jayne Mansfield over the phone. "She didn't show up. I thought she would've been working at the club today."

I hang up on her immediately. I look over at Tick and Manny. "She didn't show up to work today."

They look curiously at each other. Can't say that I blame them 'cause I don't have shit to say either.

"What about Ignacio? Eyes?" Tick turns to Manny.

"He left Rheda an hour or so after we left them. He went home and left this morning."

"She must be at the house," Tick surmises.

"Fuck it. Let's go." I round my desk and walk toward the door, with Tick and Manny close behind.

Tick drives us to the penthouse Anaya shares with my brother. We walk in to the building and toward the elevators. The doorman comes out of a back room, looking disheveled. He tries to put himself back to rights as he walks toward us.

"Sorry about that. Had to take care of something in the storage room. Can I help you gentleman?" His nameplate says Fred. I remember him from my first visit to Anaya's home. He is medium height and with a receding hairline. I think the way most would describe his look would be fatherly. Not that my father ever looked like him.

"We're on our way to the penthouse suite," Tick answers for me.

"Oh, Mr. DeLuca expecting you?"

I look at the old man and try to reserve some patience for him. He is, after all, doing his job. But I got shit to do and he is holding me back. His light gray uniform is rumpled and a bright red stain spreads across his forearm area. I lift my hand, pointing to it. "You seem to be bleeding."

He lifts his arm and lowers it quickly. "Yeah, cut myself when I was moving those darn boxes in the storage area. Couldn't find no bandages, so I did the best I could with some paper towels."

I nod at him, already moving on from this conversation. "Mr. DeLuca is expecting us."

He looks at us warily before looking in the direction of the tenant phone. "Umm, I'm supposed to call up before allowing anyone to enter." He looks down at his bleeding arm.

"Hey look, go take care of that cut before you get some type of infection, and we'll just go about our business upstairs. Mr. DeLuca won't mind." Tick, who usually turns on the charm to the ladies to drop those panties, turns it on for the doorman.

A slow smile spreads across the doorman's face. "That'd be much appreciated." He nods to us and presses the elevator button, letting us on, before typing in a passcode for the penthouse.

Tick gives a smile and a wave as the doors close. The ride to the top floor is quick. When we step off of the elevator and into the vestibule, I'm hit with the reminder of that day when Anaya stood in that doorway and threw a glass at me. Missed me by several feet, not even close. I let out a chuckle at the memory and lead the way to the door. But something is out of place. Droplets of blood make a path up to the suitcases by the door. I look over to Tick and Manny. We remove our revolvers from our shoulder holsters. I open the door and look around the living room before walking completely inside. There are smudges of blood on the furniture and floor. We hear movement in the back. I lift a finger to my mouth and walk toward the direction of the sound. The bedroom door is ajar.

I've always found the element of surprise is the best way to go when walking into an unsure situation. I kick open the door and see Ignacio standing next to a wall splattered with blood.

"What the fuck!" he yells out before his eyes settle on my own.

Rage hits me. Whose fucking blood is that? I walk into the room and spin around, looking for Anaya.

"What the fuck are you doing here?"

My jaw tightens and my fists clench. The air in the room feels like it's been sucked out suddenly. "Where's Anaya?"

"Why the fuck you asking about her?"

Tick stands next to me and places a hand on my shoulder. I fight the urge to shove it off. "The blood," I say through gritted teeth.

He shakes his head. "Not mine. We had a fight last night but it didn't leave this kind of damage."

I try to move forward but Tick holds me in place. "Be easy," he murmurs.

Easy? How can I be easy? "Fight?" I finally take in his appearance. Scratches mark his face.

"Yeah, fucking bitch was going to leave me. Saw me with Rheda. I set her straight."

"So where is she?"

He opens his hands wide. "I came home to this not too long ago. She was in bed when I left this morning." His forehead is creased as he scratches the back of his head.

I want to put a bullet between his eyes. Anaya's disappearance is the only thing that is saving him.

Manny bends to pick up the gun off the floor and smells it. "It's been fired recently." His eyes narrow as he looks at my brother.

"She pulled it on me yesterday. Didn't have the fucking guts to use it. But I sure as hell didn't fire it."

I look around the room a little more carefully. The bedsheets have dried blood stains on them. What the fuck happened in here?

## Chapter 22
### I Will Not Bow ~ Breaking Benjamin

Tony

It's been a week since Anaya's disappearance and I've been tearing up this city looking for her. Tick's connections show no activity at the airport or bus depots. It's almost as if she vanished. Manny worked with her building's security to view camera footage, but there's no sign of her leaving the building. Unfortunately, given our line of business, going to the police is just not an option. It just doesn't make sense, though.

I figured Ignacio was my best bet to lead me to her but he has been heading most of the search efforts. He's actually acting like a man desperate to find her. After several heated discussions with Tick and Manny, mostly with me threatening to put a fucking bullet in Ignacio's head, we decide to keep him alive for now. He was the last to see her and it's a strong possibility he is acting like he doesn't know where she is just to throw us off. So, I've been acting in the mindset that our plan has been compromised, which means he still walks the earth. For now.

"Tony, are you listening to me?" Winta throws her napkin at me. She cooked me my first home cooked meal in months; stuffed red snapper, with a mixed green salad and a garlic vinaigrette.

I blink away my thoughts and turn to look at my younger sister. She's holding a forkful of fish, waiting for me to say something. Anything. I've been the worst company for her and that is a shitty repayment for her kindness. "Sorry. I was just thinking. I promise to be more present for the rest of the evening. What were you saying?"

She places her untouched fork back on the plate and leans in close. "I'm worried about you. Perhaps she ran off, Tony. Maybe nothing has happened to her at all."

"The blood. The bedsheets, the room—the entire house was covered in blood. There was a gunshot in the ceiling, for God's sake. How do we explain that?"

She lowers her head and shrugs. "I don't know."

I lift my napkin from my lap and throw it on top of my plate, covering my uneaten food. "Exactly. I fear the worst and I can't let...let..." I cover my face with my hands, fighting back the weight of the tears that want to come out.

Winta is instantly by my side, holding me in her arms. "Shh, Tony, it's not your fault. None of it."

The guilt of Winta being raped and finding our mother dead from an overdose haunts my memories to this day. My life seems to be built around "if only." *If only* I had not beaten Ignacio up that last time, maybe he wouldn't have raped Winta. That was the catalyst which set off several events that changed both of our lives forever. *If only* I had not hung out with friends that day our mother overdosed, perhaps I would've gotten home in time to save her. *If only* I was honest with Anaya from the beginning, I could've saved her. This shit is my fault. My fucking decisions affect other people's lives.

My head pounds relentlessly and I'm having difficulty focusing.

"Tony, you have to hear me, once and for all. None of it is your fault. What happened to me was not your fault."

I look up, not bothering to care that I'm crying in my sister's arms. She, of all people, has seen me at my lowest points in life, this being one of them. "I caused this. I could've saved her."

"Please, I can't stand to see you like this. You're breaking my heart."

"Then what do I do?" My sister's tears fall on top of my head; perhaps I'll be baptized in them, and they'll wash my sins away. I hold my sister tighter in the hopes of being absolved of my sins.

"First, you learn to forgive yourself for things that are beyond your control." She places her hands on the sides of my face and stares deeply in my eyes. "And then, you find her, because you're the only one who can."

I've never loved my sister more than I do in this very moment. She is right. I am the only one who can find Anaya. She is so much a part of me that I know, somehow, I will find her.

# Chapter 23
## Citizens ~ Alice Russell

Tony

    I sign off on some invoices and place them in the folder. It's Saturday night at Pulse and the club is packed. I would usually be downstairs mingling with my guests and keeping an eye on shit, but I haven't been in much of a "people" mood since Anaya disappeared.

    Every day I wake up, I have to remind myself that I keep Ignacio alive in hopes of finding her. He hasn't led us to her in the two months since her disappearance. He hasn't even moved Rheda into the penthouse or vice versa. If I didn't know any better, I would think he is an innocent man. But what else could have happened to her? No credit cards, she hasn't touched her bank account, her passport was still in her luggage—it just doesn't add up.

    Even if an enemy of Ignacio's took her, we would have been dealing with a ransom situation by now. Instead, crickets. Ignacio's been drinking himself into oblivion every night. Which reminds me... I get up to pour myself another drink.

Tick opens my door and closes it behind him. One of these days, we're going to have to talk about the benefits of knocking on the door.

Lifting my glass to take a sip, I skip formalities and get straight to business. "What?"

"He's downstairs again."

No need for names. The *he* in question is Ignacio. He's become a frequent visitor of the club, usually sans Rheda. I wonder how he gets his women to be okay with that. Especially a woman like Anaya. Why would he ever want to step out on her? If I had her, I would cherish her and love her for the rest of my life. Protect her and own her, because she would be mine.

I shrug. "So?" I mean, it's not like it's anything new these days. He handles a little bit of business in the afternoon, and in the evening, he drinks and whines about shit. The next morning, he nurses a killer hangover and presses repeat.

"He's fucking with some of the customers. Bad for business and shit." He folds his arms across his chest, waiting for me to give him the okay to snap Ignacio's neck. Tick has taken exception to Anaya going missing and feels that Ignacio has outlived his usefulness.

I place my glass on my desk. "I'll handle it." I grab my suit jacket, and follow him out the door.

Sure enough, Ignacio is taunting a guest as Manny tries, and fails miserably, to diffuse the situation.

Ignacio is one of those sloppy drunks, nothing like our father. He tries to throw a punch, but the customer side steps and Ignacio falls to the floor while other patrons laugh at him. If our father was alive, he would have shot him just for the embarrassment alone.

I tip my chin at Manny and he bends to help my brother stand.

"Time for you to go home," I tell him, disgust dripping in my tone like melted ice cream.

"Hmm?" He's bleary-eyed and his head wobbles around like one of those bobblehead dolls you see on people's dashboards.

I turn to the customer. "Sorry 'bout that. Drinks on the house for you and your friends." His friends all clap him on the back, proud of him for "beating up" the drunken patron. Little do they know who this patron really is. They would piss their pants if they did. "Ignacio, time to go home. Now."

"I'll dump him in a cab," Manny says as he half-carries, half-walks my brother toward the door.

"I'll go and help him." Tick follows behind.

Tallie, our head hostess, walks over to me. "There is someone named Fred here to see you."

"Don't know any Fred."

"He insists he needs to speak to you. Kind of feel sorry for the old guy."

I look at Tick's on-again, off-again fuck buddy. "Since when do you feel sorry for anyone?"

"He kind of reminds me of my father."

There is an innocence that glows on her face, a look I've never seen her wear before. "Show him up to my office. Give me five before you do." I turn and walk off, but not before catching the bright smile that spreads across her face.

Inside my office, I take a seat with my usual drink in hand, and wait for this Fred person. I wrack my brains trying to remember a Fred, but I come up blank. My thoughts are interrupted by Tallie's soft knock on the door. I brusquely tell her to enter, already bored with the intrusion of this Fred person.

I stare at my glass as I tilt it to the left and right, the tawny liquid sloshing from one side to the other. My eyes are transfixed on it as if it is a crystal ball, hoping it could give me the secrets of where Anaya would be.

I hear the door close and a clearing of a throat. My gaze moves up to see the older gentleman standing in front of my desk. I've seen him before, but I can't place where.

"Tony?" He says my name, almost as a question as well as an accusation.

"Yeah? How do you know me?" I lean back in my swivel chair, still trying to remember where I've met him. He looks too old to be one of my regulars. Besides, Tallie would've said that. I do see what she means about his fatherly appearance. He looks harmless enough.

"We met a few times at my job. I'm a doorman, you see…"

I sit upright in my chair and place the glass on the desk. "Gray uniform, right?"

"Yes." He looks at the chairs that Tick and Manny would normally be occupying. "May I?"

I tip my chin at him and he takes a seat. *Why would Ignacio and Anaya's doorman come to see me?*

"Bet you're wondering why I'm here." He seems uneasy, not quite sitting completely back on the seat. His butt rests so close to the edge, I almost think the chair might tip over. Shit, just what I need is for this old man to tip his chair and hit his head on my desk.

"Okay, sit back and tell me your story."

He does as I ask but doesn't rest his back on the chair. "If I had known that you were someone to trust, I would've come sooner."

I'm a person he can trust? I'm a man who will eventually kill his blood brother and this man thinks I'm a man he can trust? I wonder what kind of company he keeps to think he can trust me. "I don't know about trust, but tell me what you came to say and we can determine that later." I lift my glass to my mouth and realize I haven't offered him any. "You want a drink?"

He seems to hesitate before nodding yes. "Haven't touched a drop in thirty years. My Maribelle didn't care for no liquor drinking in her house." His hands tremble as he looks down. "God rest her soul."

I walk over to the wet bar and pour him two fingers of scotch, and I debate if I should pour more. He looks like he needs the drink more than me. I hand him his glass. "Sorry for your loss...umm...Fred."

He nods and takes the glass, sniffs it, and smiles. "The good stuff." He points his index finger to his nose. "Still got a nose for it."

"Nothing but." I sit on the edge of my desk and wait for him to continue.

He takes a long sip and smiles appreciatively. Liquid courage now flowing through him, he finally leans back in the seat and begins. "I'm here because she needs more help than I'm able to give."

*She?* Maybe I misunderstood him about Maribelle. "I thought…" But then the dim light begins to brighten in my fucking thick head. The glass drops to the floor and breaks, as I stand and take a step closer to him, silently begging him to say out loud the answer I already know.

"Anaya sent me."

# Chapter 24
**Heart Shaped Box ~ Nirvana**

Anaya

*Day After the Rape…*

I hold the gun under my chin as my bedroom door slams open. I jerk my head in the direction of the door and pull the trigger accidentally. The bullet grazes my ear and hits the ceiling.

"Mrs. DeLuca." Fred runs over to me and snatches the gun out of my hand.

The will to die has left me and I haven't the energy to fight. I just need the pain to be over.

"What's happened to you?"

I stare but say nothing. I've retreated deep inside the recesses of my brain where it's safe. No one can touch me there.

"I knew something was wrong. When your town car came yesterday, when I rang for you, and Mr.

DeLuca showed up…I just knew." He lowers his head. "My God, child. What's he done to you?"

I manage a whisper. "Help me."

"I'll call the ambulance." He reaches in his pants pocket for his phone, but I grab his arm, stopping him.

"No. Pl-please, Fred. You've got to get me out of here."

"B-but…" Concern flickers in his eyes.

"He'll kill me." I manage to grab both of his arms and stare deep into his trusting eyes. "Do you understand? He'll kill me." My lips begin to tremble.

"Your husband?" His eyes widen at my confession.

I shake my fists up in the air and immediately stand. *"Not my husband!"*

He falls back on the heels of his feet, mouth agape.

"Will you help me?" I'm wringing my hands, desperate for his answer.

For a moment, I think he will say no, but his eyes soften and he stands up beside me. "Of course, I will, Mrs.... Uh..."

"Anaya. Please, call me Anaya."

"Anaya. What do you need me to do?"

For a moment, I am frozen. *Freedom? Is this really possible?*

"Anaya?" Fred's eyes widen with worry.

"I-I don't know. He said he'd kill me if I left."

"Then we'll make him think you've been taken." Fred turns and heads toward the living room. Before I reach him, he has already started tearing the room apart. He turns around to see me staring. "Quick, go shower and change. What time is he coming back?"

My head is not catching up to everything that is going on around me, and Fred ushers me back toward the bedroom.

"We got to be quick. Shower. Now! I'll finish up here. Don't wear any of those fancy dresses and shoes you normally wear. Jeans and an old t-shirt. No wording." He turns back to finish up his dismantling of my home.

I do as he says, showering and changing quickly into an old pair of jeans and a t-shirt I haven't worn in years. It's a plain black shirt, very nondescript. When I come out of the bedroom, I see Fred's handiwork in the guest rooms, my office, the kitchen, even the guest bathroom.

"I'm dressed."

"Good, don't take your pocketbook."

"I need my credit cards and I.D."

"No, leave those behind. You leave with what you got on your back."

"B-but…"

"He can't know that you left on your own. We need him to think you were hurt and dragged off." Fred turns and goes into the kitchen, coming back moments later with a butcher's knife in hand.

Instinctively, I step back. He shakes his head at me. "I'd never hurt you, Anaya. This is for me." He places the knife on the sofa, removes his gray jacket, unbuttons the bottom sleeve of his shirt and rolls the sleeve up his bicep. Picking up the knife again, he looks at me. "This is going to be the hard part, but it's necessary." With a will I never knew he had in him, he slices the knife down his arm. He bites back a yell as blood drips down. He carefully lays a pool of blood by my suitcases in the vestibule and leads a trail into my bedroom. I follow behind him, in awe of what he is doing.

"We used to have to throw the Vietcong off our trails. We did stunts like this to lure them into an ambush and kill them."

*He's done something similar before?*

In the bedroom, he smudges the wall with blood. He takes a step back and admires his work. "I think that should do it." He turns and smiles at me, as proud as a peacock. "Got a scarf? I need to tourniquet this wound."

I run to my drawer to find him one and, once again, I am amazed at yet another thing he knows how to do. When he is finishes, he goes into my bathroom and washes his hands. "We need to get out of here." I follow him out the bedroom door, thinking we're headed toward the vestibule to take the elevator down. "No, ma'am. We're going down the service exit." We walk into the kitchen and open the door that leads to the service elevator.

I've only seen this once before, on our moving day. That was how they brought our furniture up. But once again, Fred surprises me, and we don't use the elevator. He wants to play it safe and take the stairs. He runs pretty fast for a man in his sixties. Either that, or I'm pretty out of shape. Once we are down in the lobby, he hides me in a storage room, where I'll stay in there until he gets off work tonight.

I stay in the small dark space with no place to sit. I squeeze into a space on the floor and that's when everything hits me. I'm free. I'm actually free. And that's when I cry, but not tears of sadness. Tears of freedom.

# Chapter 25
## Refugee ~ Tom Petty and the Heartbreakers

Tony

*Present*

"What? When? Where? How?" My questions come out in rapid fire succession but Fred just sits patiently and waits for me to calm the fuck down. Yeah, not happening.

"She asked me to help her two months ago. Anaya, she's a good girl. Reminds me of my own daughter, Elise. She's a good girl, too." For the first time, I notice his southern drawl.

What the fuck is he talking about? Good girls? I want to talk about Anaya. "Where is she? Take me to her." I'm already grabbing my car keys from my desk.

He squints his eyes together for a moment. "I was getting to that. She's staying with me at my apartment in Astoria."

"I'll drive." I'm in a full march toward the door, but I realize Fred isn't behind me as I stand there, holding the door open. "What?"

"Not yet." He shakes his head at me.

"What the—"

"No son, you don't understand." He points to my seat and waits for me to take it.

I feel like a kid being disciplined by their parent. I drag my feet back to my desk and plop down in a huff.

"He messed her up bad. Not my story to tell. But she's not the same." He points to his head. "Nightmares, you see. If I didn't know any better, and I do, I'd say it's PTSD. Saw enough of it with my buddies from 'Nam."

What the fuck is he talking about? "PTSD? You're telling me Anaya has post-traumatic stress disorder?"

"Hmm-mmm. Mostly night terrors. She's taken to not sleeping. Won't talk much about what happened to her that night." He looks as if he is reliving a faraway moment. "She was in a state that day. She tried to kill herself."

"What?" No way, Anaya is too full of life for that.

"He snuffed the life out of that child like a flame." He snaps his finger in the air. "Oh, but some of the old her is there. She still has a beautiful smile when she remembers to use it. It's just that there isn't much I can do for her. She needs a professional. But it's not safe here, you see."

"She told you to get me?"

He nods. "Yes. She told me that the two of you have similar interests."

"Similar interests?"

"Yes, you both want Mr. DeLuca dead."

"What the fuck did he do to her?" I ask, but I know. I know it as sure as I know the sun will rise in a few hours. The memory of holding my sister in my arms after I found her bloodied and beaten and raped. Nausea hits me before the familiar bubble of rage takes its place in the bottom of my stomach. "That son of a bitch. He…" I swallow hard before finishing, "raped her, didn't he?" It's not a question; it's not even a statement. It's that thing that lingers over your head, and in your heart, for the rest of your life.

"She didn't give me all of the details. But she was pretty banged up when I found her."

"Fred. Please. You have to take me to her." It takes a few seconds before I realize this is the first time I didn't give an order to someone and expect it to be handled. I gave this man the respect he deserves for saving her.

Fred sets his glass on my desk and rises. "Guess I've told you all that I can. We should go." He walks toward the door and stops, turning to look at me. "She's lucky to have you. She'll need a man that loves her."

I stop walking, stunned by what he has said. *Love?* I don't lo—

And that's when I realize it. I do love her. How did I not know it before? When did it happen? I know that I wanted her. I want to keep her safe in my arms where she fucking belongs. But I never thought of the word *love* until now. I think it's because it's something more than love. Love can sometimes fade or end; it can even be replaced by another. But I know in my heart, what I feel for Anaya, is more than love. She is a part of me, and I guess she has been for a while now.

"Coming, young man?" Fred holds the door, patiently waiting for me.

# Chapter 26
## Skeletons ~ Stevie Wonder

Anaya

I'm sitting here, waiting for Fred to bring Tony to me, thinking about how I owe him my life, because I would have died that day had he not walked in. I honestly don't know what I would have done without Fred and his help. I want to live and I *will* fight to stay alive. But the nightmares. Every time I close my eyes, I remember that night all over again. It's on constant replay in my mind and I can't escape.

Most nights, I wake up screaming. Fred will rush into my room and rock me in his arms, telling me it will be okay. He has become so much more than a friend to me. He is like a father. His daughter Elise has been wonderful as well. She wasn't thrilled in the beginning, when she found out that I was living here, but Fred kept his promise to me and told no one. Elise eventually warmed up to me and has taken to checking in on me when her father is at work.

For the first few weeks, I stayed glued to the television, hoping to see a newsbreak about a certain crime boss being murdered in his home. But the breaking news never came and I realized I was being selfish. I can't expect Fred to take care of me for the rest of his life. I won't be safe out in the open, though, so I told him to reach out to Tony, my only hope for survival.

I look into the small mirror in the tiny bathroom and see the shell of a woman I used to be. One who has lost too much weight with hair that lays limp around her shoulders. My eyes seem to have sunk into my face and dark circles have formed around them. It's doubtful Tony would still think me attractive. But would I want him to? Sometimes, when my mind drifts to the past, I remember making love to Tony, but Iggy's face would sometimes replace Tony's, and I'd shake the memory out of my head.

It's been a tough road to recovery, physically and mentally. Every day, it's easier to cope, but I am still haunted. It's almost like being in limbo; I'm forever in between the past and the present.

When I hear a car drive down the quiet block, I always wonder if this is it. Has he found me? He said he would kill me if I ever left him. But eventually, I am able to come back to my senses and realize I am safe.

But today is different. I'm *anxious* to hear a car come down the street. One car in particular. Tony's. How did he take the news of me being alive? Did he think Ignacio killed me? How come he hasn't killed Iggy yet? Did I get it wrong? Maybe Tony has forgiven Iggy?

I begin to tremble at what could possibly be a mistake that could cost me my life. But Fred and I went over everything. We both agreed that Tony is my best bet for survival.

I hear the key turn in the lock, then the opening and slamming of a door.

"Anaya?" Fred's voice echoes through the apartment.

I step out of the bathroom and walk down the long hall into the living room where Tony and Fred stand. My gaze locks with Tony's, and I know I made the right decision. Fred excuses himself to his bedroom, closing the door behind him.

"You came." My voice is a faint whisper, and my heart pumping so hard I can hear it in my eardrums. I want to run into his arms, but my feet feel rooted to the ground.

His topaz eyes glisten. "Of course I did. Nothing would've stopped me from getting to you." I search his eyes further and I see something else in them. Pity.

I turn away momentarily, before steeling myself to look at him again. "Fred told you about what he did to me."

His eyes fall in a downward cast. "I guessed. He said it wasn't his story to tell."

I lift my jaw and stiffen my back. "I'm not broken. I've always been a survivor."

"Never said you were broken."

*Then why do I feel broken some days? How come I don't remember what it was like to be me? Who was I before? I only know what I've become.*

"Angel?" His voice is more of a plea than anything else.

My eyes snap up to meet his. "Sorry, I..."

"It's okay." He walks closer to me, slowly, then pulls me into his chest and holds me. "I'm here, baby. I'm here."

For the first time since the day Fred found me, I allow myself to cry. This time, I mourn the loss of someone close to me. I mourn myself.

## Chapter 27

### Monster ~ Eminem

Tony

My heart breaks when she collapses into my arms in tears. If Ignacio was in front of me now, I would snap his fucking neck and put a bullet in his head, for good measure. I lift her tiny frame in my arms and carry her to the worn brown couch. I instantly notice she feels like skin and bones in my arms. I sit with her on my lap and let her cry the pain away.

I don't say anything to her; she doesn't need my words. She just needs to know I am here and I will always be here for her. I stroke her back and hum "Ave Maria." My mother used to hum that to me as a little boy, when I was upset. She begins to calm down and eventually the sobs lessen until they stop completely.

I keep stroking her back, feeling her vertebrae, and a pang goes through me. That fucking bastard did this to her.

"Don't stop," she murmurs into my shoulder.

"Hmm?"

"Don't stop humming." She lifts her head up and shifts so she can look at me.

"Sorry, I didn't realize I'd stopped." I give her a weak smile. "Why didn't you come to me sooner? I would've gotten you out of there."

She stands and sits next to me, taking my hands into her cold ones. "I wasn't thinking clearly. I didn't know who to trust anymore. Between what you told me and finding Rheda with him… It was too much."

"Angel, I'm so—"

She places her finger over my mouth.

"Don't apologize. This isn't your fault."

"But if only I killed him before, he wouldn't have had a chance to…to…"

"Rape me?"

"This is on me."

"No. It's on him." Her expression darkens.

She says "him" almost as if she is afraid saying his name will conjure him in front of us. I want to exorcise those demons for her, only I won't use a cross and holy water. I'm thinking, a bullet and a shovel.

"I kept him alive in hopes of him leading me to you." I say this as if I am in confession. Can she wrap her arms around me and forgive me?

"That's why?" she whispers. "I've watched the news for months." Her voice trails off. "Fred, of course, is afraid to mention him to me. He doesn't want to bring it all back to me. But what he doesn't understand is you can't bring it back if it never left."

"Angel. Fuck. I swear on my mother's grave, I'll kill him."

She rises and walks to the window. Her movement is so graceful she looks as if she is floating. She places her hand on the glass overlooking the street below, and I listen to her breathing. Inhale: one, two, three. Exhale: one, two, three. I keep listening until my breaths mirror her own.

"Tony, I used to think that is what I wanted. I often daydreamed of it. When I sent Fred to get you, that was one of the things on my mind. For you to kill him. If he was dead, then it would heal me. If he was dead, then I could sleep at night. If he was dead, my life could go on." She turns around to face me. Her still beautiful eyes look too large for her slim face and sunken cheeks. "But for some reason, just now, when you said it, I realized something. Killing him won't help me move on."

"You don't want me to kill him?"

"I'm not saying that. I'm saying don't kill him because of me. You need to make peace with your own past the way you see fit. But don't do anything in the name of what has happened to me."

I rise and walk toward her. "Then tell me. What can I do to make this better?" I already know the answer. I've lived through this with my sister.

"You being here. You came to me when I needed you. That's all I can ask for."

*It's now or never asshole, don't fuck this up.*
"Angel…" No, I want to say her name when I say these words to her for the first time.

She stares at me with her wide eyes, waiting for me to finish my sentence.

"Anaya, I'll always come to you. When you disappeared, I fucking thought I was losing my mind." I close my eyes, trying to figure out the right words. How do I explain that I couldn't breathe when she wasn't around? How do I say if she died, I died? I exhale. "I'm fucking this up. I've been fighting this for so long but after speaking to Fred tonight, it finally got through my thick head." Her bottom lip begins to tremble. "Anaya, I love you. I don't know how else to explain everything that I feel for you other than to say there is no me without you. I should've said it to you the night of the charity ball. I panicked, as usual. But I felt it, and I just didn't know how to say it."

Tears fall down her cheeks and I feel like I've been sucker-punched. I fucked it up, after all. I rush to her and take her into my arms. "Angel, I'm sorry. I'm not saying it right. I'll get better at this. I-I promise. It's

278

just, I've never said I love you to anyone besides my mom and sister before." My words stumble out of my mouth like a teenage boy who ejaculates too early his first time.

She lifts her hand and touches the side of my face. Her hands feel soft against my skin. "It was perfect."

"B-but you were crying."

"I know. It was because you were the first man to say that to me."

"H-he...ugh." I don't even want to say his name. "He never told you he loved you?"

She shakes her head and lowers her eyes. "Oh, God. I never realized it until now." She places her hands over her face. "How could I be so stupid?" She lifts her head up and her eyes are moist. "Why did I stay?" A soft sob escapes her mouth. "Why didn't I leave a long time ago? If I left years ago...this...this wouldn't have happened."

I grab her and pull her into me. "Angel, it's not your fault. Do you hear me? It's not your fault." I repeat these words to myself as well. Hopefully, I'll believe it isn't *my* fault, either.

Chapter 28

## Don't Let Go ~ En Vogue

**Anaya**

I wake with a start, sitting up in Fred's daughter's old twin bed. The shades are closed so my eyes have a hard time adjusting to the darkness in the room. Only a little bit of sunlight peeks through the sides. Even though her old room has become my room over the past few months, I am always startled by my surroundings when I first wake. Looking around the room, my eyes and mind try quickly deciphering I'm safe. My racing heart steadies when my eyes settle on an old poster of Michael Jackson, from his "Thriller" days. Somehow, seeing him in what is now an iconic black suit, hat, and bedazzled white glove, feels like home.

I stretch out the kinks in my muscles from sleeping on the thirty-year-old mattress and yawn, instantly realizing the bed only has me in it. Tony stayed with me and held me, even though the bed was too small for his large frame. I fit perfectly in his arms as he held me tight and whispered that he would never let me go. My fingers instinctively reach out to feel the pillow that is still wet from my tears.

Standing up, my feet touch the worn linoleum panels on the floor. In spite of the chill in the air, the floor is warm. The door is ajar and I lean closer to see if I can hear his voice down the hall in the living room. I hear murmurs but am unable to distinguish what he is saying. I turn to look at the clock and the bright red numbers read ten-forty-five a.m.

*I slept that long?* I'm so used to barely sleeping each night. Pushing the door fully open, I walk down the long hallway, passing Fred's bedroom, which I notice is empty and the bed is made. In the living room, Tony's back is to me as he talks on his cell phone.

"Get Manny and meet me at my office in four hours." Pause. "I'll text you her address so you can keep a guard at her door." Pause. "And Tick?" Pause. "I want him dead. I'll do it myself if necessary." He ends his call and tosses the phone on top of the four-seater dining table.

He stands, his feet bare, in an unbuttoned, untucked dress shirt. His back muscles flex as he runs his hands over his face and through his hair in frustration. My heart becomes so full from the sight of him, and I feel guilty for burdening him with my troubles.

"Tony." My voice sounds so small compared to all the trouble surrounding us. Such a small boat in the middle of a tsunami.

He turns around with a startled look on his face, but his eyes soften when they meet my own. "Angel. Sorry.

Did I wake you?" He walks toward me, concern written in his strong features.

I shake my head. "Just missed you, that's all. Everything okay?" I want him to do what Iggy has never done. I want him to share with me. Open up and lay himself bare for me to see.

He purses his lips for a moment before speaking. "Do you really want to know?"

"Yes, please. Talk to me."

He takes my hand and we walk to the worn, brown plaid couch and sit. "I spoke with Tick and gave him the update on you." He pauses a moment, looking away.

"You told him what he did to me, didn't you?" My voice is soft, not accusing, filling in the gap for what is hard for him to say.

He looks down before admitting, "Yes. I'm sorry. I felt that I had to tell him so he knows the urgency."

"It's okay. You don't have to walk on eggshells around me." His face relaxes a bit and he kisses my forehead. Deep down inside, I wish he'd take me in his arms again and kiss me with the wild abandon he used to. Perhaps even take me to bed and make love to me. But another part of me is unsure if I'd even be able to do that. Would I ever be able to make love to him again? This will forever be the third party in our relationship. Will Tony be able to stand the rain with me?

"I won't. I promise you." He squeezes my hands and then lifts each hand to kiss. His lips are soft and warm against my skin.

"You have to leave me for a few hours," I murmur.

His eyes widen. "You heard."

I nod.

"I'm leaving someone here with you. I'll be back in a few hours. Just have to…"

"Kill him?" I refuse to say Iggy's name out loud. I have an irrational fear that if I say his name too many times, he will appear in front of me, ready to make due on his promise to end me.

"The less you know, the better it is for you."

"You're doing it today?"

"Not sure, that's why I'm meeting with Tick and
Manny."

"What happens if you don't?" My hands cover my
trembling knees.

"You start packing your stuff. You'll stay with me.
I'll pick you up when I come back." He isn't asking me,
he's telling me, just the way Iggy used to. It was always
assumed he'd speak and I'd listen—no, *obey*. I'd obey as if
I was one of his flunkies, but my days of obeying are over.

"No." Tony blinks rapidly at my response, his
mouth slack. "When you come back, we will discuss all of
the options. I'm not leaving one situation just to get back
into the same mess." I've read that doing the same thing

repeatedly and expecting a different result each time is the definition of insanity. And I'm far from insane.

"Angel, you're safer with me."

"No, I'm safer on my own. Tony, you're a dangerous man. Violence begets violence." I've read that also. Since being in hiding, I've had a lot of time on my hands, and reading is one of my vices.

"Angel, it seems to me that is what you need right now. A dangerous man to kill another dangerous man."

I stand to walk away from him.

"Anaya, I'm the man who will die for you. Kill for you. Protect you. I won't apologize for it. Being around me shouldn't bring thoughts of violence. Not when you know I'm more than that."

"I know." I lower my head.

He stands in front of me and lifts my chin. "Angel, I love you. If you want to talk about the living situation when I get back, then we can do that. You want to stay here, that's fine. I'll just make arrangements with Fred about me staying here with you." His lips brush against mine. "I finally got you back. I can't live without you again."

His lips fully connect with mine and he draws me in. My arms wrap around his neck and I make a silent promise to myself to never let him go.

He cups my face in his hands and leans his forehead against mine. "I don't want to leave, but I have to."

"I'll be here." *Waiting.*

His head turns toward the window and he nods slightly before turning back to me. "Got a man outside now. His name is Pearce. If you have any problems, just yell for him."

"I'll be fine. Go. It's not like I'm going anywhere." Already, I feel alone and lost. I don't want him to leave. Tony back in my life is like me finding my sense of true north.

He doesn't let me go. "Maybe, you should come with me."

"No. Go. I'm fine."

He hesitates for a moment longer but I push him in the direction of the bedroom. Reluctantly, he walks down the long hall, me following behind.

"Do you have a cell?" he asks as he sits on the bed and starts putting on his socks and shoes.

"No. I left everything behind. There's just the house phone."

Tony's eyebrow perks up.

"Yes, Fred believes in house phones." I turn to grab a notepad and paper. Jotting down the house number quickly, I hand it to him.

He places the paper in his wallet. "When I come back, I'll bring you a cell."

"I really don't need one. It's not like I go out or anything."

"This phone will have a GPS system and panic button. Just in case you need me. I told you. Never losing you again."

## Chapter 29

**Firestarter ~ Prodigy**

Tony

I walk through the doors of Pulse and see Tallie, along with a few others, wiping down some tables in preparation for tonight's crowd. She looks up and smiles.

"Hey, Tony. Tick and Manny are already waiting for you in your office. And Chelsea is upstairs in one of the VIP rooms with some workmen."

Chelsea took over where Anaya left off with the club redesign.

"Okay, no visitors until we're done." I wave at a few people as I walk to the private elevator.

When I enter my office, Tick and Manny are already seated and waiting for me. Manny is playing Words with Friends on his cell, and Tick, well he's just being his typical broody self.

Manny barely spares me a glance as he concentrates on beating his opponent. "What's good?"

Tick kicks his foot out, knocking into Manny, causing him to drop his phone.

"Fucker. You did that on purpose," Manny complains as he bends to pick up his latest iPhone. He is forever purchasing the newest iPhone, sneakers, and Polo gear. Guess he could have worse obsessions.

"Pay attention, fuck face," Tick growls out.

Manny places the phone in his pocket while grumbling out, "I *was* paying attention."

I take a seat behind my desk and look at the two of them, wondering if I need to intervene, and decide against it.

"How's Anaya?" Tick turns his focus over to me as Manny, who is still mumbling under his breath, gives him death glares.

"As good as can be expected, under these fucked up circumstances."

"I picked up that phone for her you asked for. Already loaded it with the security shit." He tosses the box onto my desk. I lift it up.

"Thanks for this."

He shrugs. "No prob."

"Let's get to the business at hand. Ignacio has outlived his usefulness to us. I have Anaya back, so let's discuss options."

"You want him dead, so we bust a cap in that ass," Manny quips and then stretches, letting out a loud yawn that sounds like Chewbacca.

"Tact, asshole. We need a plan or shit can get messy real quick." Tick stares at me as he speaks to Manny.

Those two have a big brother-little brother type of relationship, and I usually find myself mediating for the two.

"Well then, what's the plan?" Manny lights up a cigarette, takes a deep drag, and puffs out a ring of smoke. A satisfying smile spreads across his face, like he just busted his load.

"That's what we're here for." Tick turns to him and growls.

Manny flicks cigarette ash into a glass on my desk and mutters something unintelligible.

I shake my head at the two of them. "Did you work out a truce with the Jersey crew?"

"Yeah, they feel the same way we do. He's no longer needed." We discuss my brother as if we're discussing the balance sheet on a report.

"Good. Don't want any blowback."

"I got this shit covered. Definitely no blowback."

"Logistics?" I ask.

"He'll come to the club tonight as he usually does. The Jersey crew will take care of the rest."

I mull over his words for a minute. This has been the plan all along. We went over these details in depth before. But the reality of it hits…I'm about to kill my brother.

"Tony, you alright?" Tick asks.

I clear my throat before responding. "Yeah. I'm good. Guess this is it."

Tick settles back in his seat. "Yep, by the end of the week, this shit will be over. Back to normal."

*But what the fuck is normal?* My life has been so consumed by the hatred of my brother that I don't know what the fuck normal is anymore. When I got up each morning, I knew my purpose. Now, I'm not sure what that purpose is supposed to be. Then Anaya's beautiful face comes to mind, and I know my purpose going forward; to love and protect her. Fuck the rest. Nothing will get in between that.

I check the time and decide that I've been away from Anaya long enough. "We'll pick this up later."

"Headed back to Astoria?" Tick surmises.

"Yeah, got some more things I need to discuss with her." I stand and grab the box Tick handed me minutes ago. "I'll be back tonight. Keep me posted."

Tick stands. "I'll walk you out."

Manny rises and walks to the door that is slightly ajar and opens it completely. Holding it open, Tick and I head down the hall with Manny in tow. The heavy scent of a woman's perfume wafts the air around us.

"Shit. That Chelsea sure knows her perfume. I would fuck a bitch without looking at her just from the scent alone," Manny says as he closes his eyes and inhales deeply.

"Yeah, she always had a thing for those expensive French perfumes," I reply absentmindedly, my sole focus being Anaya.

We take the stairs and see Tallie standing at the bottom step, waiting for us. "You have guests. I put them over there." She points to one of the lounge areas where four men are seated with drinks.

I look over at Tick. "Thought you said you had shit handled."

He shrugs. "They might be here for some other shit. Let's go and talk to them."

I see Chelsea gathering up some things and placing them in her large purse.

"Oh hey, Chels. Didn't get a chance to check in on you. How's it going upstairs?" I ask.

Startled, she looks up and brushes a hair away from her face. "It's going great," she replies, walking over to us.

I look at the cell phone box in my hand and curse. I'm supposed to get back to Anaya. No telling how long this meeting will take, so I yell out for Kenny, our bartender-slash-anything I need him to be. He stops what he's doing and jogs over to me.

I hand the box to him. "I need you to deliver this."

Tick reaches into his pocket and pulls out his car keys. "Here." Kenny takes the keys, smiling that Tick is trusting him with his prized possession. "Drive easy." That's funny coming from the speed demon's mouth. "I'll text you the address and details."

Chelsea stares after Kenny's retreating back before turning back to me. "Looks like you are really busy. The workmen know what to do. And I've gotta run. Call me if you need anything." She zips up her Louis Vuitton bag and swings it over her shoulder. Chelsea is already a tall woman but in her stilettos, she looks like an Amazonian. Her heart-shaped ass looks like it is going to burst out of her too-tight skirt as she rushes toward the door, looking almost like a duck waddling.

"Alright, let's get this meet and greet over with," I grumble and lead the way to the table of our Jersey guests.

# Chapter 30
## Baby Did a Bad Bad Thing ~ Chris Isaak

Tony

The meeting with the Jersey crew is over and that's four hours out of my life I'm never getting back. I've had appointments with my dentist to get my tooth pulled that were more enjoyable than this. At one point, when I couldn't take any more of their "what if" bullshit, I nearly said, "what if I put a bullet in your asses," but Tick was able to sense my temperament and ease their questions.

Kenny came back all smiles, happy I trusted him with an important task. He's been itching to become a main member of my crew. I just might give him a chance; he seems like a capable kid. I'll have to remember to talk to Tick about it later.

\*\*\*\*

I look at my Tag Heuer watch and realize it's a little after midnight and my brother hasn't shown up yet. I'm starting to get annoyed at his absence because I'm much later getting back to Anaya than I wanted to be. I signal for Manny, who is talking to some women. He pats one of them playfully on the ass and walks over to me.

"What's good?"

"He's not here. We still got eyes on him?"

He takes out his cell and dials. "Where is he?" he speaks into the phone. I stare at him and wait. He hangs up and looks at me. "He hasn't come out since we dropped him off last night. He had a few visitors."

Nothing odd in what he is saying, so I turn my attention to looking for Tick. "You seen Tick?"

"Tony, you might want to listen to who the visitors were."

My back stiffens when he says this, just as my eyes settle on Tick, talking to Chelsea across the room. Chelsea has become a regular at the club since taking over the design project. She usually sits at my brother's table. She is such a power-hungry whore, she decided it would be in her best interest to become my brother's drinking buddy on his nights at the club.

"Okay, who?" Tick leans into Chelsea, his hand on her waist. She throws back her head and laughs at something he said, her platinum hair bouncing around her shoulders.

"Rheda."

Rheda, not a big deal. She stops by to fuck him or get him to sign some paperwork. "And?" Chelsea places her hand on Tick's shoulder. I can tell he's getting ready to take her home for the night. I look over and see Tallie glaring at them.

"Wheeler and Jay." Manny's tone is cautious.

I shrug. So what? Wheeler and Jay are his main men. No big deal. I'm bored with this fucking conversation. Nothing new for him to report. I'm about to walk away, when he says a name I can't hear. It's at that time Chelsea turns around and our eyes meet. Her lips glisten in her favorite shade of red. Her smile is wide and her eyes are alluring. She would fuck me and Tick together if I wanted.

Manny places a hand on my shoulder but I'm too caught up in what's happening to really notice. I stare into her eyes as everything around me fades away. A frown forms on her lips for a fraction of a second, before it's replaced with a smile. She is no longer looking at me but through me, and that's when I know who the other visitor was.

My feet are moving before my mind registers what I'm about to do. Pushing through the crowd, my eyes never once leaving hers, each step I take brings me closer.

Standing in front of her, Tick tilts his head in wonderment.

I can barely contain my rage when I ask, "What did you do, you fucking bitch?"

# Chapter 31
**In-A-Gadda-Da-Vida ~ Iron Butterfly**

Anaya

*6 hours earlier...*

A nice, soothing hot shower is what I need—besides that, Tony should be here shortly, and I don't want him to see me still in my pajamas this late in the afternoon. I look at the neon green numbers displaying the time on the cable box. Six-fifteen. Where did the time go?

Fred should be home shortly and I haven't made dinner. He always complains that I am spoiling him, but it's the least I could do for all that he has done for me. I rarely cooked before, when I lived in the penthouse, but now I find cooking helps to take my mind off of things. It's never anything over the top but it makes him happy, and it's a comfort for me.

I go into the small galley-style kitchen and pull out the chicken I had marinating and set it on the stove to get room temperature before I bake it. My stomach grumbles a little, and I realize I haven't had anything to eat since my lunch of beef lo mein Tony's bodyguard brought for me to eat.

Pearce is not as intimidating as Tick and Manny, but from the qualifications he rambled off to me, he seems to be more than qualified to keep Ignacio's men away from my doorstep. Perhaps I'll invite him upstairs to eat with us. Tony shouldn't mind that and it would ease my conscience of having someone sitting outside in a hot car looking out for the boogeyman.

I'm staring into the fridge, trying to decide what to take out for our vegetable course, when the doorbell rings. I flinch at the sound and wait. Pearce told me he would do two short, followed by two long bells, to let me know it's him. The other ring doesn't come and I grab a steak knife before running toward my bedroom. I hesitate a moment longer, my heart now in my throat, and beads of sweat form on my forehead.

"It's Kenny. Tony sent me," a voice calls through the locked front door.

*Kenny?* I don't know a Kenny, and Tony would've told me about him. I walk to the window and see Pearce's car. Because of the tree, I can't tell if he is sitting inside or not. I grab the phone extension in my room and dial Pearce's number. He answers on the first ring.

"What's up?"

"Someone is at the door."

"Be right there." He hangs up and within a few minutes, I hear yelling outside my door, followed by the doorbell signal Pearce taught me earlier.

I stall, not sure if I should trust this. But then the house phone rings, and I answer it without saying anything, waiting for the person on the line to speak.

"It's me, Pearce. You can open the door. Tony sent Kenny to drop a box off to you."

I exhale loudly and run to the front door and open it. There stands Pearce, who is about five feet ten inches, and, I'm assuming Kenny, who towers over him, and looks like he is sixteen.

"Sorry, Tony did tell me to go through Pearce first. I forgot and came up with your downstairs neighbor, who let me in."

"Tony sent you to me?" I narrow my eyes at him, still not sure if I can trust him.

"Yes, he said that he will be running late. Asked me to give you this." He hands me a cell phone box. "He said that it's fully loaded."

"Oh." I look at Pearce and he nods. "So, he's not coming?"

"He said he's running late. That's all I know."

Pearce looks at Kenny. "You should get going before your shift begins at the club."

"You work at the club?" I'm more shocked because, seriously, he can't possibly be more than sixteen or seventeen.

"Oh, yeah. Been working for him since the beginning." Kenny puffs out his chest, which I assume he thought was showing muscle but, instead, it's just showing bones. "I know I look young for my age. Bet that's what you were wondering. I get that a lot."

"Kenny, go. You're boring her, and me."

"Oh yeah, I'll go. Sorry about the confusion. If you don't mind, can you keep that between us?" He smiles innocently.

"Umm, sure. I guess." I look at Pearce, who rolls his eyes.

"Thanks. See you later." He waves and leaves.

"Sorry about that. I know that must have been scary. It won't happen again." Pearce lowers his head.

"It's okay. I'm going to take a shower really quick and cook dinner. You're more than welcome to join Fred and me."

He shakes his head and holds his hands up. "No. I keep watch downstairs till Tony gets here. But thanks for the offer." He turns toward the door. "Call if you need me." And with that, he leaves.

I open the box and stare at the iPhone. It looks

unassuming. Will this really work in terms of safety? I look

at the clock again and realize that time is running out to

cook dinner. I go to the bathroom, carrying the phone in my

hand absentmindedly. My robe is hanging on the bathroom

door and I place my new possession in its pocket. My long,

soothing, hot shower will now turn into a five-minute

wash-up, since I am running low on time and Fred should

be walking through the door any minute now.

I shower as quickly as possible in the small claw-

footed tub. Sometimes I miss my large shower at the

penthouse, but not the life that came with it. I'll take this

over anything else. I turn off the shower and listen to the

pipes make loud banging sounds. The first time I took a

shower here, that sound scared me so much, I fell out of the

tub. I've long become accustomed to the sound now and

it's comforting.

I reach for my towel and dry off, trying to listen for Fred in the living room. He usually comes home and turns to MSNBC to watch the political shows he loves so much. But there's nothing. Perhaps his train was just late. Stepping out of the tub, I lotion up and grab my terrycloth robe. Fred's daughter, Elise, bought it for me my second week here. Because of the unintentional weight loss, it has steadily grown larger and larger in size. It can just about wrap around me twice at this point.

The bathroom lights flicker and I let out a groan. That darn circuit breaker again. The building is very old, so if you run too many appliances at the same time for too long, it taxes the breaker.

I knot my robe as I walk down the hall, through the living room to the kitchen. Flipping the switch has become such a normal part of my routine. But I know the house by heart and can easily find my way without an issue.

I step in something wet. *What the hell?* I look up at the ceiling and wonder if Fred's neighbor's washing machine overflowed again. My feet slide in the warm puddle, and I reach out to catch my balance on the wall but touch someone instead. Before I can yell, a hand goes over my mouth and the lights come on.

There lies Fred, steps from where I stand, lying in a pool of his own blood.

# Chapter 32

**Numb ~ Linkin Park**

Tony

*Present*

Tick releases his hand from her waist and stands, waiting for me to give him a signal. She turns around to look at him before turning back to face me.

Her Botox lips form a smile. "Tony. What on earth are you yelling about?" She takes a step closer to me and plays with my lapel. "I guess I can forgive you for calling me a bitch, given our long history together."

I grab her wrists and give her a shove. She stumbles backward into Tick's chest. He sets her back to rights. "Don't give me that bullshit. What did you tell Ignacio this afternoon after you left the club?"

Her eyes widen and she blinks rapidly. "I went to his house to make sure he was okay. He was pretty drunk last night."

"He's been worse in the past few months and you haven't bothered to check on him before."

She gives me her best resting bitch face. "So what? I decided to check on him now. What's it to you?"

"Chelsea, you and I both know you don't do shit unless it benefits you. You overheard my conversation, didn't you? Then you saw an opportunity."

Her lower lip trembles and she wrings her hands as if she is trying to pull an answer from them. I move on to the next question.

"How much does he know?" I think I know this answer too, but I ask anyway.

She refuses to look me in the eyes, which is all the answer I need. Everything. She gave him everything.

"Couldn't stand to pass up a quick dollar." She opens her mouth but I keep talking. "I'm just surprised you didn't start a bidding war between me and him. You disappoint me." I sneer at her and watch her face fall.

Her moment of weakness only lasts a millisecond before the fighter in her comes out swinging. Chelsea glares at me with her feline-shaped eyes.

Yeah, she's a fucking cat alright. This bitch always lands on her feet. Or so she thinks.

"Fuck you, Tony. So what? I saw an opportunity and I decided to make a dollar from it. Besides, he won't harm her or anything, he loves her."

"Love? That's what you call it?" I get in her face, Manny standing close behind to pull me away if needed. In case I snap her damn neck. Which, in all honesty, I just might do.

Her eyes widen with fear as I breathe fire into her face—bared teeth and all. "Let me tell you what he does for love." I lean into her ear so only she can hear me. From the outside, it would look like an intimate moment between us. "Instead of the tender caress of a lover, he prefers a fist. Or maybe, in his sick mind, he would call it love taps. For foreplay, he enjoys binding their hands and feet as he brutalizes them in ways that would make Ted Bundy blush. When he's done, he makes them beg for it again, and again, and again." I pull back to see the tears streaming down her face, giving her the appearance of a raccoon. I lean into her other ear to finish the story of my twisted fucking brother. "He tells them if they run, he'll find them. If they talk, he'll kill them. And do you know why?" She shakes her head. "Because he fucking *can*."

She is trembling so hard, I have to hold her to keep her from collapsing onto the floor.

"So, tell me, Chelsea. Is that love? I guess some might call it that. I just call it by the name that it deserves: rape."

"B-but…" Her Botox lips remind me of that press conference with Leona Helmsley, when she was crying. Pathetic and unsympathetic, from my view point.

I look at Tick. "Call Pearce, now."

He dials the number and stands there with the phone to his ear before shaking his head. *No answer.*

"Where would he take her?" Manny walks from behind me and stands by my side.

"One of his warehouses?" Tick asks, while redialing Pearce.

"N-no." Chelsea's voice is faint over the loud beat of the music. "He would take her to my storage warehouse."

"How can we trust you?" Manny steps in closer to her.

She stiffens at his question, the fight back in her again. "Because you don't have a choice."

# Chapter 33

## She Began to Lie ~ Greg Hale Jones

Anaya

I wake up slowly. My head hurts. I try to lift my hand and touch my head, but my hands are tied behind me. What's happened to me? My head is foggy, as if I've been drugged. The last thing I remember is heading to the kitchen to turn the breaker back on, and then...and...the leftover beef lo mein I ate for lunch rises in my throat, threatening to come out.

Fred. He's dead. His gray hair a horrific shade of red as he lay in his own blood. I did this to Fred. He would still be alive if it weren't for me. Elise, his daughter; the pain she will be in when she finds out. They were so close. I've destroyed their family. I begin mourning the loss of a dear friend who was more like a father to me than my own. He didn't have to help me when he did, and now, this is how his good deed is rewarded. I can almost hear Fred's voice in my ear, telling me to stop feeling sorry for myself and fight to live. If I don't fight to live, then his death is in vain.

*Anaya, you've got to focus. You have to fight to stay alive, and you will mourn Fred when you are free.* Where am I? Ignacio must've found me, but how? Did I put my trust in Tony when I shouldn't have? Wait, Tony. The phone! I shift my hip and feel the weight of it in my pocket, and a tear falls down my cheek. *All is not lost.*

Tony should be able to find me. I just need to stay alive long enough. But then I remember I never turned on my phone. When Kenny handed it to me, I simply placed it in my robe pocket. Fuck! If I can get my hands out of these ties, I can power it up so he can find me. I struggle against the binds and they cut into my wrists. I've felt worst pain before, so I keep wriggling my wrists in hopes of the ties loosening.

*What is that sound?* I stop what I am doing and listen. Is that my imagination? Footsteps. It sounds like footsteps coming closer. A lock. It's the sound of someone unlocking a door.

"Hello?" I call out into the darkness, trying to keep the fear from my voice. Lights flicker on immediately, and I blink a few times to let my eyes adjust. A figure is standing in front of me. I try and look up to see who it is, but I can't; my head hurts too much.

"Welcome back, baby," an all too familiar voice rumbles through my soul.

"Ignacio?" I ask, as fear takes hold of me.

"Who else were you expecting?" he responds as I watch his feet, one step at a time, come closer to me. The tension within me tightens like a coil.

I close my eyes, wishing the fogginess of my brain would disappear. I still feel drugged and my thoughts are not coherent. It's possible I'm imagining this, but my eyes are open and I'm staring at the same Italian leather shoes I bought him for his birthday. "Why am I here?" The question comes tumbling out of my mouth.

"I asked *you* a question, my love. Were you expecting someone else?" Malice is evident in his voice.

"No. I don't typically expect to be kidnapped." Except by him, perhaps. I try to angle my neck to get a look at him, but a sharp pain slices through me and I stop trying.

"Kidnapped? I call it a reunion."

*A reunion?* "You didn't have to kill Fred." I bite my bottom lip, preventing me from ending the sentence with, "you sick fucking bastard," the way I initially intended. Now is not the time to pick a fight with him. Fear has left me, replaced by anger. Sheer unadulterated anger. It flows warmly though my veins and I welcome it wholeheartedly.

"A casualty of war." He sits on the floor in front of me, carelessly crossing his legs, as if he were about to toast marshmallows at a campfire.

My shoulder feels numb from laying on it against the hard concrete. I try to shift the weight from my shoulder to my back, but my bound legs prevent that. "Ignacio, can you please untie me?"

He reaches out his hand and places a loose hair behind my ear, as if he was a tender lover. "You used to call me, Iggy."

*Yeah, I used to call you Iggy when I thought I was in love with you. Before you raped me and stripped away my dignity and freedom.* He took so much from me in that one night, and now, he looks to take more from me. My life. Well, fuck him; he won't take that from me. I'll play his stupid game until I see an opportunity. "I'm sorry. Iggy, my arms are numb. Can you please untie me?" My eyes slowly move up from his knees, and up his body, until they meet his dead gaze.

His hand strokes my hair and face gently. "Two months and seventeen days." His voice is low and I strain to hear him.

It takes me a moment to realize what he means. That was how long I disappeared for. I open my mouth to speak but change my mind and decide to listen for now.

His touch is soothing yet terrifying at the same time. "I didn't know what happened to you. Thought you were dead. Thought they...took you." His voice cracks at the end, tears form in his eyes. "I was about to drink myself to death and you were, what? Playing house?" He grabs a fistful of my hair and yanks my head back. His eyes are now narrow slits. I let out a yelp as my roots burn from the pull.

Warm tears fall down my cheeks. I stick my tongue out and taste the salt from them. "I knew you would find me." The words rush out of my mouth, reminding him of the game we used to play with each other. His fingers loosen their grip on my hair and I feel the tension in my scalp release.

He lays on his side in front of me and tries to pull me in closer, but my knees block him. He frowns like a child and looks at me. "One sec." He rises to his knees and unbinds my hands and feet. The rush of blood flows through them, sending sharp tingles into each appendage. I flex my hands and try to move my feet to gather the feeling.

He pouts at me and I realize my faux pas. Without much feeling in my legs, I sit up and move in closer to him, wrapping my arms around him. "Thank you, Iggy. I always knew you would find me, again."

He inhales, stroking my hair, and places my head against his chest. "Always. I'll always find you."

I realize, for the first time, that the Iggy I've known all these years is insane. How had I not seen it before? I need to figure out a way to get out of here. "Let me show you how much I love you," I whisper into his chest. He stiffens and stops stroking my hair.

"Yes. I'd like that."

We both sit up and, with as much courage as I can muster, I lean in and kiss him. He attacks my lips and I try not to puke in his mouth. I move my lips down his chin and to his neck, sucking, marking him the way he used to like. Eventually, I am able to pull away from him and hold on to the belt of my robe. His eyes wander down to my hands as he waits for me to untie it. I seize my chance, and rear my head back, hitting him hard in the nose. Blood shoots out and I am momentarily dazed. He falls backward and I see my opportunity.

I run for the door but he grabs my ankle and yanks with all his might. I fall forward with flailing arms, trying to break my fall. I land with an *umph,* the air leaving my lungs in a swoosh, my chin hitting the concrete. I bite my tongue and the metallic taste of blood fills my mouth as I fight back a cry. The door swings open with a loud bang and I see a woman's heels walk in. She bends down, and I see her face. *Rheda.* She picks up my phone that fell from my pocket when Ignacio grabbed me. Holding the phone up and looking at me, she says, "Guess you won't be needing this," just before she throws it against the wall. The back cover comes off and I hear the shatter of the screen, along with my hopes of getting out of here alive.

# Chapter 34
## Killing Strangers ~ Marilyn Manson

Anaya

"Why is she untied?" Rheda snaps at Ignacio as she bends to pick up his gun, aiming it at my head.

I sit up and watch the scene unfold before my eyes, waiting for another opportunity I hope will come my way.

"Didn't see a need to keep her tied."

"Didn't see a need?" She throws her head back and laughs. "That's why I'm the brains. You leave that shit to me to think about."

I angle my body so I can look at his expression. He looks like a child who has been scolded. *She's been controlling him all along?*

"Give me your belt." Her palm is out, pointing towards me.

I look down at my belted robe and instinctively place my hands on the knot.

"Since when are you so modest? It's not like it's anything he hasn't seen before." She shakes her hand in annoyance.

Reluctantly, I undo the knot and feel the fabric release from around me, cold air hitting my skin. I throw the belt in her direction. She grabs it and stands, walking behind me, and ties my hands behind me. I instantly feel the blood circulation stop.

"How could you, Rheda? I trusted you!"

Rheda stares at me, not a single sign of remorse on her face. "It's not like you knew what to do with a man like Ignacio. He's better off with me."

Even I wouldn't wish a man like him on a backstabbing, lying bitch like her. "You fucking cunt." I try to stand but she gives me a hard shove. I fall onto my bound hands and cry out in pain.

"Oh, poor Anaya," she taunts me. "'*Ignacio ignores me, he doesn't touch me anymore.' Poor Anaya grew up without a family. Poor Anaya, always so weak and helpless!* Just once, can you get a backbone?"

I struggle against my restraints, hoping to free my hands so I can choke this bitch. A sharp pain shoots through my shoulder and I cry out again. "But what about you? Pretending to be my friend while fucking my boyfriend?"

"Oh, she finally grew some claws?" She claps her hands together slowly, mocking me.

I'm so fucking angry, I could spit bullets at her and pierce her stone-cold heart. But then a thought hits me, and I realize I have something that she doesn't, that she never would. "Do you want to know why he untied me?" I finally wiggle my way to my side and slowly sit up on my knees.

"Shut up," he yells.

She looks at him and her face falls.

"He still wants me. Not you. Think about it. You know it's true." Tony's words come back to me. "He cried for me every night. You couldn't fill my place, could you? No matter how hard you tried." *Keep talking, Anaya.* Perhaps I can buy myself some time to come up with a plan.

Her bottom lip trembles. "You're lying."

"Am I? Really? Look at his neck and tell me if that's the way you left it." I stare at her with a smirk on my face.

Her eyes zero in on the mark that I left on his neck just minutes ago. "You fucking bastard."

Gunshots echo in the warehouse. Instinctively, I drop to the ground.

"Stay with her," Ignacio instructs. "I'll see what's going on." I hear the sound of the door opening and closing, and then Rheda and I are alone.

I lift my head and look to Rheda, who seems frozen in place. "Untie me," I plead.

She blinks at me, as though slowly realizing she's still in the warehouse. "I can't." Her voice is a wobbly hush.

"Yes, you can. You're going to risk your life for a man who doesn't give a shit about you? I thought you were smarter than that, Rheda. What happened to that headstrong lawyer I know? You're going to let him play you?"

"B-but…" her voice quavers.

"If you untie me, perhaps I can talk Tony out of killing you, too. You know that's him out there." I meet her gaze.

"I'm not afraid to die." Her hands shake as she aims the gun at my head, once again.

"Not afraid to die? Really, Rheda? You're okay with dying for a man who would pass you over for me?" I hear the click of the safety. Those were the wrong words. Then I remember her sister Haylee. "You're willing to die for a man that raped me?"

"You're lying," she whispers, but she knows I'm telling the truth. I can see the pain darkening her expression.

"You would be dishonoring Haylee's memory if you did."

She turns away from me. Echoes of gunfire sound in the distance. *Does Ignacio have more men in*

*the warehouse? Who's here? What do they want?*
Ignacio bursts through the door, breathing hard, gripping the holster of a Glock. He scrambles over and pulls me against him. "Come with me," he rasps into my ear. He drags me behind him, then forces me into the larger room.

The scene before me steals my breath. It looks like a Mexican standoff of sorts, with a group of men, their weapons drawn and trained on us.

"Wait! Don't shoot!" Tony's voice roars out as he slowly walks forward. He looks from me to Ignacio before his eyes finally settle on Ignacio's gun trained on my head.

"I *will* shoot her!" Ignacio yells, his hand shaking violently. I say a silent prayer that he doesn't accidentally pull the trigger.

"No!" Tony holds up his gun. "Take me instead. Let her go and take me."

Ignacio's body shakes and I hear guttural noises spewing from his mouth. "It was you all along. Hitting my shipments and warehouses. I trusted you. You're supposed to be my brother! Where's your loyalty?"

"We stopped being brothers the moment you raped Winta."

"It was rough sex."

"You raped her to get even with me. Looks like Father won after all. He twisted your sick fucking brain."

"You always took what mattered most to me. Father's love and now her love, too?" He gives me a hard shove and I stumble forward before he snatches me back to him, his hot breath in my ear. "Tell him you still love me. Tell him." His voice cracks and his spittle lands on my face.

I turn my head to look at Tony and then back to Ignacio. I see Rheda standing a few feet behind him. Her eyes are bloodshot and she seems unsteady. The gun in her hand looks too heavy for her to hold, even limp by her side. She raises the gun as our eyes lock. The look that passes between us seals our fates. In that moment, I feel a generosity that he has never shown me and I give him what he needs to hear. "I love you, Iggy." I close my eyes, warm tears falling down my face.

The sound from the gunshot makes me yelp out loud, only to be drowned out by the echo of the shot throughout the warehouse. I open my eyes to see Iggy's widened ones before he collapses onto the ground, dragging me with him. I land on my side, unable to move because of my bound hands. Iggy's face is turned toward me, and he's gasping for air. Dazed, I'm unaware of the commotion around me, listening only to the sound of my still beating heart.

"Angel, are you alright?" Tony is by my side and he unties my hands, helping me to sit up before taking me in his arms and kissing me.

"Thank you," I whisper, unable to say more because I'm crying. *I'm alive.*

Ignacio coughs and my breath catches at the sound, suddenly aware that he is also still alive. I turn around to look at him, dying on the cold concrete ground. I glance at Tony. "I have to go to him."

He looks hurt but nods and lets me go. I rush to Ignacio's side and kneel before him. Holding his hand in mine, tears fall down his face. He coughs again and I wipe the blood from his mouth. He tries to speak but I can't hear him. Leaning in closer to understand, his final words will haunt me till the day I die: "I knew you would find me."

# Chapter 35
## Maybe Tomorrow ~ Stereophonics

Tony

Standing over my brother's lifeless body, watching Anaya and Rheda sobbing, I try to gather my thoughts. All these years, I've hated my brother for everything he's taken from me. I thought I'd be overjoyed, relieved at his death, but in actuality, I feel sadness. He ruined so many lives because of his twisted mind. But what about all those years I wasted hating him, my own brother, and not letting people close for fear I might lose them as well? He didn't do that to me. I did that. I let him control my life, my actions...all these years. And I didn't realize it until this moment.

"Tony?" I hear my angel's voice calling for me. She is standing next to me, eyes wide like an innocent child. I pull her into my arms.

"Angel, are you alright?" I ask, searching her face. What's going on in her head? She just watched the man she's been with for twelve years die right before her eyes.

"Shouldn't I be asking you that question?" She's frowning, and her brown eyes flash concern and sorrow…for me. She grips my face in her trembling hands. "Are you alright?"

Am I? I don't honestly know. What does one do when the object of their hate is dead? Do they find someone else to hate? Every morning since my mother's death, I woke with one purpose: take down Ignacio. Make him pay for all he's done. For years, Ignacio was my purpose. He's dead now. I'm at a loss…what's my new purpose?

I place my head on Anaya's shoulder and she holds me.

"It's okay. It'll be okay. I love you, and we'll get through this together," she whispers in my ear.

That's when I realize *she* is my purpose. Anaya is my reason to get up in the morning. She is my reason for living. Whatever anger and hatred I had in my heart has been replaced by love for this woman. I wrap my arms around her, embracing her, letting her know I'm here for her as well.

My angel looks at me and squeezes my hand gently before releasing it. She kneels beside Rheda, bracing her arm around the sobbing woman's shoulders. Rheda's eyes bulge at first, but she soon collapses in Anaya's arms.

"Tony, I got some people on their way to take out the trash," Tick announces from behind me. Thank God for Tick and his efficiency.

# Chapter 36
## Radioactive ~ Imagine Dragons

*Two Weeks Later*

Tony

Rheda has taken a leave of absence from her job in order to process everything mentally. Anaya has tried offering Rheda her support, but Rheda has shut her out.

I'm so proud of my angel. She could've hated her former best friend for everything, but she found room in her heart to forgive Chelsea, Rheda, and even Ignacio.

First thing on my list is to marry her. I cannot imagine my life without Anaya as my wife.

Because Ignacio's men requested a sit-down with me today, Tick and I walk into a warehouse similar to the one where Rheda shot my brother dead two weeks ago. Ignacio's men are already waiting. I take a seat at the table and Tick sits down to my right.

"Okay, you requested a sit-down. I'm here, so let's get this over with," I say, commanding authority. I have better things to do with my time. Like crawl back into bed with my angel and listen to her scream out my name.

A large man with a shaved head and tattoos around his neck clears his throat to initiate the meeting. "With Ignacio gone, there're *disagreements* over who should be the head of the DeLuca family. Since you're old man DeLuca's son, we thought the privilege should go to you."

"All your men are on board with this?" Tick asks, his tone even, his gaze piercing and alert.

"Yeah. If Tony doesn't take the reins, the in-fighting can get bloody. I'm trying to prevent that," Shaved Head answers, his voice gravelly.

"Here's the thing. I'm going legit. I'm turning all my current holdings into legal enterprises. If I take the DeLuca reins, I'll do the same there. The first couple of years won't be as lucrative as you're used to, but once all the businesses are legit, the cash will start flowing again. If your crew agrees to those terms, then we can talk. If not, then there is nothing left to say," I say, clasping my fingers together as I lean on the table.

Ignacio's top lieutenants discuss amongst each other. Tick and I watch and listen to the murmurs. I had a feeling Ignacio's men would want a sit-down with me. Tick and I were already prepared to take any and all necessary steps. Either turn everything legit, or burn it all to the ground.

Shaved Head tips his chin, signaling the end of their private discussion. "You have yourself a deal." He stands up and walks over to me, shaking my hand. "I'm Magnum, by the way."

The other lieutenants follow suit. Eight of the ten lieutenants shake my hand. I look over to Tick who has noticed this slight as well.

Tick and I pull Magnum aside. "Not all of your lieutenants are on board," I say to Magnum.

"Yeah, those two, Jay and Wheeler, they're against it," Magnum responds, cocking his head in the direction of the two holdouts.

"They going to be a problem?" I already know the answer to this question, but I want to see if Magnum is going to keep it straight with me.

"Yeah. I think they might be a problem. It'll depend on how their men take this news," Magnum replies, looking me in the eye.

*Good, I like it when someone doesn't bullshit me.* "Alright then, you've just become my eyes and ears. I expect you to work with Tick on making this transition as smooth as possible. You take Tick's word as my word. When you have proven yourself to me, you will get a larger role."

"I can respect that," Magnum says, before heading in Jay and Wheeler's direction. I like this guy. A straight shooter and not big on words, just like Tick.

"We expected a few holdouts," Tick reminds me.

"Yeah. Just surprised it was only two," I say thoughtfully.

"You trust this guy?" Tick asks, indicating Magnum with a tip of his chin.

"For now, yes, but keep a close eye on him. Let's see how things develop."

"You ready to get out of here?"

I take a look around at each of the men. I'll have my work cut out for me but I'll get out on top. I have to; there is so much riding on my success. Not to mention, I have Anaya counting on me, and that is all the motivation I need.

"Yeah," I say. "I have a girl waiting at home for me. And I have an important question to ask her."

## The End

# A Letter from the Author

Dear Reader,

Thank you for reading this book and taking this journey with me.

I know certain parts of this book were hard to read as it touched on topics of rape, domestic abuse, and violence.

I do not condone rape or any form of abuse or violence. If you or a loved one are a victim of abuse or rape, I beg you to speak to someone about it. No one should have to go through this alone. I implore you to reach out to a help center. Please remember, you are not alone.

Victims of rape, please call: R.A.I.N.N (Rape Abuse & Incest National Network) (800) 656-HOPE (4673)

Victims of domestic violence, please call: The National Domestic Violence Hotline (800) 799-7233

All the best,

Autumn Sand

# ACKNOWLEDMENTS

Thank you to all of my readers who took the time to read this book. As some of you may already know, this is a complete rewrite of the original book. I added some characters and changed some storyline plots. The reason for the rewrite is because I learned from my reviews what I was lacking in some areas. Never doubt the power of a review.

I want to say a special thank you to Britta Neal for helping me as my personal assistant. Tracy Willoughby of Broken Chicks Escaping Reality Through Books, who reached out to me after she read the second book of this series, Mayhem. Her kind words helped me to finish this book that I didn't have the energy to complete.

Thank you, Jenn Wood, my editor, who has become the guiding force in my writing effort. The following incredible authors that I have befriended and I've learned so much from, Sandra R. Neeley, Callie Press, Sienna Grant and Scarlet Wolfe. Thank you to Tracy Arnett from Spunky and Sassy and Tina Franzen Spurlock from Little Shoppe of Swag for their advice.

As I get older, I learn and I grow each day, but one thing I'll never grow out of is my need for my mom. My heart is full with thanks and appreciation for her and for standing behind me. Last but not least, I can't forget my cheering squad, Carl Kent from Powersmith Studios, Richard Rauch, Lucious Anderson and Melanie Cameron.

# About the Author

Autumn Sand was born and raised in New York City. With her love of restaurants, her shoe fetish, and her hard-nosed heroines, Autumn is a New Yorker, through and through. Autumn has a shoe collection of 300, and the credit card statements to prove it. Other than shoe shopping, she has various interests, such as: reading, writing, and traveling. Autumn has worked in the fashion industry for most of her adult life, and recently decided to pursue her dream of writing sexy, thrilling, romantic suspense. She's reluctant to call herself an author but considers herself a person who writes words that people just so happen to like to read. Autumn has a sarcastic sense of humor and loves to make her friends laugh. She enjoys a good glass of wine, but her go to drink of choice is a Jack and Coke with a twist of lime. None of those froufrou girlie drinks for her.

Autumn loves to hear from and interact with her readers.

Find her online!

**Facebook:**

https://www.facebook.com/Autumnsandauthor/

**Street Team:**
https://www.facebook.com/groups/1525475377477822/

**Twitter:**

**https://twitter.com/autumn_sand**

**Goodreads:**

https://www.goodreads.com/autumn_sand_author

**Website:**

http://www.autumnsandauthor.com

**Amazon:**

https://amazon.com/author/autumnsand

www.ingramcontent.com/pod-product-compliance
Lightning Source LLC
Chambersburg PA
CBHW071305200626
46813CB00015B/132